Poetry: A Very Short Introduction

VERY SHORT INTRODUCTIONS are for anyone wanting a stimulating and accessible way into a new subject. They are written by experts, and have been translated into more than 45 different languages.

The series began in 1995, and now covers a wide variety of topics in every discipline. The VSI library currently contains over 600 volumes—a Very Short Introduction to everything from Psychology and Philosophy of Science to American History and Relativity—and continues to grow in every subject area.

Very Short Introductions available now:

Available soon:

For more information visit our website

www.oup.com/vsi/

Bernard O'Donoghue

POETRY

A Very Short Introduction

OXFORD
UNIVERSITY PRESS

OXFORD
UNIVERSITY PRESS

Great Clarendon Street, Oxford, OX2 6DP,
United Kingdom

Oxford University Press is a department of the University of Oxford.
It furthers the University's objective of excellence in research, scholarship,
and education by publishing worldwide. Oxford is a registered trade mark of
Oxford University Press in the UK and in certain other countries

Published in the United States of America by Oxford University Press
198 Madison Avenue, New York, NY 10016, United States of America

British Library Cataloguing in Publication Data
Data available

Library of Congress Control Number: 2019941405

ISBN 978-0-19-922911-6

Printed in Great Britain by
Ashford Colour Press Ltd, Gosport, Hampshire

Contents

Acknowledgements

I am deeply grateful to my kind and long-suffering editors at
OUP—Luciana O'Flaherty, Andrea Keegan, Jacqueline Baker,
Deborah Protheroe, and, above all, Jenny Nugee who has helped
hugely with the later stages with good humour and decisive
skill—and to my invaluable copy-editor Dan Harding. I have
been talking to people about poetry for most of my life: most
extensively to my students at Wadham, Magdalen, and Somerville
Colleges, Oxford. In the distant past I had inspiring teachers:
Joe Garvey, Barney Quinn, Bernard McGarry, and Wallace
Robson. I can still feel the excitement of the sound of poetry
projected by Dan Donovan at Presentation College, Cork
who tempted me away from engineering towards *Macbeth*.
Conversationalists I remember with particular gratitude are
Nuzhat Bukhari, Catriona Clutterbuck, Joe Foweraker, John
Fuller, Adolphe Haberer, Keith Hanley, Joseph Hassett, Nick
Havely, Catherine and Marie Heaney, Mick Henry, Ellen Hewings
and her daughter Nancy, Geraldine Higgins, Alan Hollinghurst,
Matthew Hollis, Mick Imlah, Fr Matt Keane, Rosie Lavan, TaoTao
Liu, Tony Lurcock, Jamie McKendrick, Andrew McNeillie, Ankhi
Mukherjee, Cliona Ní Riordáin, David Norbrook, Séamus
Ó Cróinin, Tom and Josie O'Donoghue, Stephen Regan, John
Rigby, Steven Rose, Fiona Stafford, Robert Young, and first of all

my sisters Eileen and Margaret. In the old days there were smoky discussions into the early hours in a Park Town garret with David Williams, Tom Paulin, and Desmond O'Brien. My most sustained conversation on poetry and everything else has of course been with my wife Heather to whom I am endlessly grateful.

List of illustrations

Introduction

Is poetry important? Certainly grand claims have been made for it: the English Romantic poet Percy Bysshe Shelley ended his *Defence of Poetry* in 1821 with the ringing claim that 'Poets are the unacknowledged legislators of the world'; and the first sense in *The Oxford English Dictionary (OED)* recognizes the 'exalted' nature of poetry, defining it as 'imaginative literature as a whole at its most exalted'. But the *OED* also recognizes a familiar, more explicit and practical sense:

> 2a. The art or work of a poet. a. Composition in verse or some comparable patterned arrangement of language in which the expression of feelings and ideas is given intensity by the use of distinctive style and rhythm; the art of such a composition.

In considering the later history of poetry in English the more conceptual sense has been particularly authoritative since Shelley's time when such terms as 'sublime' or the *OED*'s 'exalted' have been used to acknowledge this higher claim. But it is necessary to make some linkage between the two senses—the written poem as verbal practice, and the grand thought of which it is claimed to be an expression. Are there clear criteria by which we can recognize that a particular piece of poetry belongs to the 'grander' category? One factor here is scale: nobody would deny the great classical epics, the works of Homer and Virgil, their standing as major instances of poetry and as historically significant; but how do we adjudicate between shorter writings? In his 1880 essay 'The Study of Poetry' the Victorian critic and poet Matthew Arnold proposed that readers should have in their minds a series of 'touchstones'—that is, pieces of writing whose greatness is agreed, against which other works can be tested to evaluate their worth. As an example of something which possessed an incontestable claim to poetic depth, T. S. Eliot proposed a line given to Piccarda Donati in the third canto of Dante's *Paradiso*, the third and final part of his *Divine Comedy*, completed in 1320 and widely considered one of the great works of world literature. She is describing the relationship to God of the blessed in heaven:

E'n la sua volontade è nostra pace. (And in his will is our peace.)

In fact Arnold had used the same line as a touchstone of excellence three times in the course of the twenty-two pages of 'The Study of Poetry'. Where might we look for such excellence in English poetry? A. E. Housman in *The Name and Nature of Poetry* in 1933, one of the most attractive English analyses of poetry, proposed these lines from *Macbeth*:

> Duncan is in his grave;
> After life's fitful fever he sleeps well.

This, Housman says, is poetry for which 'there is no other name'. But how do we recognize or define such a quality? The end of Keats's 'Ode on a Grecian Urn' has had its proponents (though also its sceptics):

> 'Beauty is truth, truth beauty'—that is all
> Ye know on earth, and all ye need to know.

2

This *sounds* true, expressed in the generalizing form in which grand truths are often couched. But *is* this all we need to know on earth? Is the proposition itself true? And does it matter if it's not? It has sometimes been suggested that poetry belongs to the realm of the general truth while prose is concerned with the particular. But particularity has also been praised as a virtue in poetry: some greatly admired lines are very context-bound, such as the opening of the poem 'Stopping by Woods on a Snowy Evening' by the American poet Robert Frost:

> Whose woods these are I think I know.
> His house is in the village though.

Pronouncing on the nature of poetry and defining it is, then, a complex and disputed matter. But some recurrent oppositions might be noted at the outset. First of all, in the Western tradition (which of course is not the whole story) from the Greeks to the present day the most fundamental distinction is between the idea of poetry (and art more generally) as either imitative, or transcendent: either imitating life or reality or nature, or surpassing those things in a way that somehow compensates for their deficiencies. The distinction is expressed beautifully in the title of M. H. Abrams's great book on English Romantic poetics, *The Mirror and the Lamp.* In its attempt to reconcile the two fundamental views of poetic operation, the title offers an elegant imagery for the two functions: poetry as a mirror that reflects reality, by Aristotelian imitation of an existing source; or as a lamp, something independent of the external world that shines a new and perhaps transcendent light on it. The Aristotelian idea of art as imitation is most famously expressed in English by Hamlet: 'To hold, as 'twere, the mirror up to nature'. But is poetry imitative or imaginative/creative?

Much of the discussion of poetry can be conducted with this opposition, including for example the fundamental debate in

3

English between Wordsworth and Coleridge to which I will return, over whether there is a distinctive language of poetry. Not if (like Wordsworth) you believe that the role of poetry is to describe things by imitation 'in the real language of men'; but there must be such a distinctive language if (like his friend Coleridge) you believe poetry depends on an inspired, transcendent faculty of imagination which will require its own language.

As well as what poetry *is*, the other crucial question is what poetry is *for*: whether it has a duty of public utility and responsibility. This was Shelley's view when he made the famous claim we began with, for poets as 'the unacknowledged legislators', a role which clearly implies a sense of public responsibility. On the other hand, there is Auden's view that 'poetry makes nothing happen', which presumably liberates poets to go their own way while conceding their public insignificance.

Poetry's obligations

But how well equipped is poetry to take on responsibility for public pronouncement? In the 20th century, Czesław Miłosz asked a sombre question in his poem 'Dedication': 'What is poetry which does not save | nations or people?' Can a poem, it was asked in the same period, stop a tank? Such despair about the effectiveness of poetry was not new in the 20th century, particularly terrible though that century was thought to be, prompting as it did Theodor Adorno's bleak declaration that 'to write poetry after Auschwitz is barbaric'. When the German critical philosopher Martin Heidegger asked in the mid-20th century 'What Are Poets For?' his title was echoing the poem 'Bread and Wine' by Friedrich Hölderlin at the end of the 18th century: 'and what are poets for in a destitute time?' Clearly, this question of social or political effectuality is at the heart of the matter; even Plato said that there was no war in Homer's time which was conducted or advised or brought to a successful

4

conclusion by him. If poetry is worthy of the grand claims made for it, including a claim for universality, it must meet such high political demands as were made for it in the 19th century by John Stuart Mill and be of use in times of crisis.

When the poet/playwright Vaclav Havel became president of the Czech Republic in 1990, his first address on New Year's Day attempted to refine the defeatist view of politics as the art of the possible, saying 'let us teach ourselves that our politics can be not just the art of the possible...but that it can even be the art of the impossible, namely the art of improving ourselves and the world'. Havel's high-minded, poet's view was fiercely opposed; but as well as being a noble programme for politics, it is connecting with a traditional, exalted view of poetry. In his celebrated disquisition on 'The Poet', given as a lecture in 1842 and published two years later, Ralph Waldo Emerson declared that 'poetry was all written before time was' and that 'the birth of a poet is the principal event in chronology'. Sir Philip Sidney in his *Apologie for Poetry* (*c*.1579) said poetry was the 'first light-giver to ignorance'. On this view, poetry exists as something equivalent to nature, and the poet is the sensitive instrument that responds to this pre-existent thing to produce a poem. At the end of his lectures collected as *The Use of Poetry and the Use of Criticism*, T. S. Eliot makes the same kind of claim for the prehistoric nature of poetry, saying 'hyperbolically one might say that the poet is *older* than other human beings'. We are reminded of Walter Pater saying of the 'Mona Lisa' that 'she is older than the rocks among which she sits'.

So, as urgent as the dispute about whether poetry is defined by its formal elements or its transcendent qualities is the debate about the rights, wrongs, and obligations of poetry—whether it is obliged to be concerned with public matters. In the late 1930s, the German poet-playwright Bertolt Brecht's poem 'In Dark Times' ends: 'they won't say: the times were dark | Rather: why were their poets silent?' After all, if Shelley's claim for poets as the unacknowledged legislators is to be taken with any seriousness, then some attention to the affairs of the world seems essential. Shelley's word 'legislators' is a forceful one: not just people whose writings have to be politely taken into account, but authorities who make binding laws of some kind. Pater, Emerson, and Eliot all claim a long prehistory as part of art's claim to authority; perhaps this is what needs to be acknowledged as giving poetry the right to legislate.

It has to be conceded too that legislation of the kind that Shelley is exalting is an idea that is dependent on political power. Insofar as there is any real truth in his heady proposition, the legislators of the world in the 19th century are likely to be already distinguished by class and sex. The extension of the legislature to women writers or writers of marginal political class or ethnicity has been a slow process, though in the later 20th century poets such as Judith Wright, campaigning for Australian aboriginal rights, and Maya Angelou, an American civil rights activist, expressed strong and effective political views in their poems.

So the question of whether an established sense of ethical responsibility and capacity are what poetry is fundamentally for can still be raised—what is the social utility of this phenomenon which, as we will see, seems to exist in all societies? The necessity of moral motivation has also commonly been questioned: poetry not only cannot but should not be involved in public debate. Coleridge defines a poem as 'that species of composition which is opposed to works of science by proposing for its *immediate* object pleasure, not truth'. In Seamus Heaney's *Station Island*, a fictional James Joyce tells Heaney to please himself rather than to see poetry as the pursuit of virtue. 'You lose more of yourself than you redeem, doing the decent thing', he tells him. So is poetry at liberty to please itself, to be in Yeats's fine word 'self-delighting', in keeping with Coleridge's view that its primary function is to delight rather than to instruct? If it does revise its ambitions in this way, presumably it is forgoing Shelley's claim to legislate for the world.

In England debates about the duties and freedoms of poetry were first conducted in the Elizabethan period when the Puritans' strictures on the irresponsibility of the poets prompted the response of the Apologists such as Sidney's *Apologie* and a bit later Ben Jonson's *Discoveries*. In the influential introduction to his anthology of *Elizabethan Critical Essays*, G. Gregory Smith goes as far as to say we should be grateful to the Puritan haters of poetry (he uses the remarkable Greek term *misomousi*) for provoking the sympathetic arguments of the Apologists for it. Concerns with the duties or freedoms of the poet were much discussed again in the 1930s in England. The Irish poets Louis MacNeice and his contemporary C. Day-Lewis (they later modified their position) argued sternly for 'Impure Poetry'—poetry that gets its hands dirty with public matters, even if that is doing 'the decent thing'.

We find the grand Romantic claims to authority often bluntly dismissed by their successors, like MacNeice and Day-Lewis's collaborator Auden who, writing his great elegy for Yeats, said 'poetry makes nothing happen'. Already in the Romantic period itself, Keats in a letter to Reynolds on 9 April 1818 was sweepingly dismissive of the public answerability of the poet: 'I never wrote one single Line of Poetry with the least shadow of public thought.' On the other hand, many Romantic contemporaries of Shelley took the view that poetry was reprehensible in eschewing public engagement.

Shelley's Romantic claim for the transcendent authority of poetry can be widely paralleled in other eras ever since the classical past. The most authoritative classical predecessor in raising the question is the Latin poet Horace who said that the function of poetry, broadly speaking, is to instruct, *prodesse* rather than *delectare*, to please. It is a choice which is certainly more significant than the matter of writing in verse forms or not, and one which has had a greater centrality in the discussion of poetry through history. Is the function of poetry primarily to instruct or to amuse? If it is a matter of instruction, this might warrant the grand authority Shelley ascribes to it. Sidney, without advancing the same claim for legislative authority, had declared that 'of all sciences ... is our poet the monarch', intending 'the winning of the mind from wickedness to virtue'. So the obligation of public answerability in the poet may be seen as a subsection of poetry's general requirement of a sense of responsibility and moral worth.

But is the poet obliged to tell the truth at all, whether morally improving or not? Poetry makes things up. In his *Apologie* Sidney made a famous—and ingenious—claim, that 'the poet nothing affirmes, and therefore never lyeth. For, as I take it, to lye is to affirme that to be true which is false.' Both its advocates and its detractors agree that poetry can be fictive. In 1766, Richard Hurd—who was influential in his time—said that poetry entails three things: figurative language, fiction (that is, non-dependence on what is demonstrably the case for its acceptance), and versification. Its fictiveness can be either a virtue—a requirement of the Romantics' theory of the imagination, and an essential for the American poet Wallace Stevens; or it can be a failing, according to Plato and Jeremy Bentham. Bentham's utilitarian view in *The Rationale of Reward* (1825) is particularly forcefully put: 'The poet always stands in need of something false ... Truth, exactitude of every kind, is fatal in poetry.' Long before, the Greeks held strong views about the moral standing of the poet: according to Diogenes Laertius, Pythagoras claimed to have seen in a vision Hesiod and Homer being tortured in Hades for their irresponsible lies: Hesiod screaming in pain, attached to a bronze pillar, and Homer hung from a serpent-infested tree. Heraclitus declared that Homer deserved to be flogged.

Sidney saw pleasure and instruction as inextricable motivations in poetry—'teaching through delighting'; but many poetic traditions have seen pleasure as the more important. For instance, the Chinese text known as the *Classic of Poetry* (1100–600 BC), which is said to feature the world's earliest example of rhymed verse, celebrates the pleasures of sexual love among the things with which poetry is concerned. In returning to ask what the duties of the poet are, it is striking once again how recurrent this question of poetry's functions and duties is across widely separated cultures and eras. And it is a fundamental question that we find addressed throughout the history of English poetry, from Chaucer's *Canterbury Tales* with their division into stories of 'sentence or solaas' ('moralizing or comfort') to Sidney in the passage I have just quoted, to the Romantics, and modern sceptics like Philip Larkin.

Might ethical motivation then be what poetry is primarily for—the validation in social utility of this phenomenon which seems to exist in all societies? Of recent books on poetry in English, the one that makes the case for its public responsibility most passionately is the volume on *Poetry* in the Oxford University Press series 'The Literary Agenda', by the poet and Hölderlin scholar, David Constantine. His last two chapters are called 'The Office of Poetry' and 'The Public Good', and they start from an observation by Czesław Miłosz: 'Never has there been a close study of how necessary to a man are the experiences which we clumsily call aesthetic.' This observation is the heart of the matter: in requiring a sense of the public good in poetry (Chaucer called it 'common profit') the demand is not necessarily for engaged involvement in the politics of a particular time, but for an awareness of the importance of the world beyond the poet.

Such awareness is what entitles poetry to be taken seriously. From the time of Aristotle to the European Renaissance, it has been said that a view of writing that linked to philosophy outweighed mere artifice in writing, however skilled. Much as he admired Chaucer, Arnold regretted that his lack of what he called 'high seriousness' (*spoudaiotes* in Greek) disqualified him from inclusion among the very greatest poets. Formal skills associated with metrics, scansion, and the like were relatively low-valued as the arts of the journeyman writer, while the concern of the serious commentator was with the field of enquiry that the method was applied to.

The universality of poetry

Ezra Pound said 'Poetry is a composition of words set to music. Most other definitions of it are indefensible or metaphysical.' Anthony Storr's inspirational book *Music and the Mind* begins: 'No culture so far discovered lacks music. Making music appears to be one of the fundamental activities of mankind; as characteristically human as drawing and painting.' The same seems to be true of poetry (which of course has close connections with music); all cultures practise it, whether or not they have writing systems. Furthermore, this phenomenon seems to enjoy a universally high status; in the words of the Russian American poet Josef Brodsky, 'poetry is the supreme form of human locution in any culture' (*On Grief and Reason*). The American Serbian poet Charles Simic says '[my] view is that poetry is inevitable, irreplaceable, and necessary as daily bread. Even if we were to find ourselves living in the crummiest country in the world, in an age of unparalleled vileness and stupidity, we'd find that poetry still got written.' The same point had been made more engagingly in Sidney's *Apologie for Poetry* which competes with Shelley's *Defence* for recognition as the most attractive of the English anatomies of poetry, when he salutes the 'great passport of Poetry, which in all nations at this day, where learning flourisheth not, is plain to be seen; in all which they have some feeling of Poetry', even 'in our neighbour country Ireland, where truly learning goeth very bare'. In the same period George Puttenham in *The Arte of English Poesie* (1589) says that in all nations there is 'some feeling of poetry'.

The most famous claim for universality in poetry was made by Goethe in a much-quoted letter to Johann Peter Eckermann in 1827 where he proposed the notion of *Weltliteratur*, world literature—an idea which has had a great deal of attention in the early 21st century. Goethe writes:

> I am more and more convinced that poetry is the universal possession of mankind, revealing itself everywhere and at

all times in hundreds and hundreds of men...I like to look
about me in foreign nations, and advise everyone to do the
same. National literature is now a rather unmeaning term;
the epoch of world literature is at hand.

But this universal occurrence of literature does not mean that
the form it takes, or what it is understood to be, is the same for
all ages and societies. So Goethe says it is necessary to 'look
about...in foreign nations' because no single version of poetry
or literature is to be thought predominant or the model for all.
'We must not give this value to the Chinese, or the Serbian,
or Calderon, or the *Nibelungen*'; but, despite this salutary warning
against any kind of ethnocentrism in the definition of poetry,
Goethe concedes that 'if we really want a pattern, we must always
return to the ancient Greeks, in whose works the beauty of
mankind is constantly represented'. This grounding of literature
on a Greek foundation has been central to the definition of poetry
in the Western tradition. It was particularly marked among the
Romantics: in his Preface to *Hellas*, Shelley said 'We are all
Greeks—our laws, our literature, our religion, our arts have their
roots in Greece'. This bias demoted even the Romans (presumably
including Horace, with his cherished pronouncements on poetry,
among them)—Shelley adds: 'But for Greece, *Rome*...would have
spread no illumination with her arms.' But we still have to bear in
mind the prejudices that this veneration for Greek carries with it:
David Hawkes, writing about Chinese poetry, warns us that
'no guarantee of universality ever attaches to generalizations about
European literature. We [Europeans] are all, as it were, Children
of the Book; all have passed through the winepress of Aristotle.'
We must, as Goethe himself said, look beyond the Greeks 'in
foreign nations' and cultures.

An even more problematic concern about world literature is
that the limitations of coverage extend well beyond the issue
of Greek dominance. Poetry occurs everywhere; but in the era of
globalization, the poetry of much of the world does not get

examined at all. For example Arabic poetry is recognized where it intersects with—and influences—the love poetry of the European Middle Ages. But there is much less awareness of the active and popular modern tradition of communal oral poetry in the contemporary Arab world. It can be described to speakers of English, but not analysed by them. This problem is even more marked in the poetry of Africa. Throughout this book I return to consider the parallels and contrasts with Chinese poetry because it is a detailed poetics that has been extensively described in English, though it often has a very different view of what poetry is and how it is written. At several points it has intersected with and influenced poetry and poetics in English, notably in the American tradition, with Ezra Pound and the poets of 'Mind and Landscape' anthologized by David Hinton. But we must not forget that an introduction to 'poetry' which is itself written in English will only ever scratch the surface of the range and depth of what 'poetry' is and does worldwide.

The claim for universality then is a commonplace in the discussion of poetry and its origins: perhaps only music—or love—has been as wide-ranging a theme. But there is a kind of sociologist's dilemma in this general claim, like the problem encountered by the American linguist Edward Sapir when he remarked that the grammatical structure of newly studied Native American languages shared its semantic organization with familiar European languages: but how could we know what its organization is without understanding the language? Is it not a presumption based on the structure of languages that we know? Similarly, how can a society like ours which has, and prizes, a practice it calls poetry, be sure that it is not simply superimposing the qualities and values it attaches to its own poetry on to some different phenomenon in an unfamiliar society? This unease arises pointedly in the terminology used by Brodsky and Simic above: Brodsky's 'locution'—use of spoken language—is not definitive. Even more doubtfully, can we always speak of poetry, in all societies, as 'written', as Simic says? Clearly we cannot deny the name of poetry to anything that is not written—the history of the ballad in English and Scots, for example, is testimony to this.

To rephrase the question, then: are we sure that Chinese poetry is the same kind of thing as English or French poetry? Moreover, does the word poetry, translated word for word, mean the same thing as *poésie* in French, or *poetria* in Latin, or *filíocht* in Irish, or *Dichtung* in German? Does it refer to exactly the same thing as *kavita* in Hindi, or *mashairi* in Swahili, or *ewi* in Yoruba? Is the Greek *poiein* the same as the medieval Scots *makyng*? Is there some identifiable common element underlying the connotations and nuances of all these words? Sidney wondered about the universality of these 'making' words: 'I know not whether by luck or wisdom, we Englishmen have met with the Greeks in calling him a maker.' In practice though, when we look at the definitions of poetry in different cultures we will find that, as in the naming of the constellations or the formulating of the rules for courtly loving, there is a surprising degree of overlap: Brodsky's view that poetry is language at its most intense and compressed, for instance, is widely encountered. Miłosz notes this improbable piece of universality: 'One of the strangest regularities to be taken into account by a historian of literature and art is the affinity binding people who live at the same time in countries distant from one another.'

This is particularly striking in looking at Chinese poetics in relation to the European tradition: even when the poems are so unfamiliar in their written forms that it is difficult for a translator to know how those forms relate to meaning at all, the concern with what poetry *is* raises very similar issues. For example, in the *Analects* of Confucius it says of *The Book of Poetry* in the course of the remarks about it from which his view of poetry is deduced: '*Poetry* can serve to inspire emotion, to help your observation, to make you fit for company, to express your grievances, to teach you how to serve your father at home and your prince abroad, to enable you to learn the correct names of many birds, beasts, herbs, and trees.' Most followers of Confucius would describe poetry as primarily a matter of moral instruction; but we can see its coverage had a range of the kind we are familiar with in the Greek tradition too.

Such universalizing claims for poetry of course raise questions of representativeness. Just as the underrepresentation of women writers came to mind in considering who Shelley's legislating poets might be, similarly the canon of world writing must be explored more widely before the phrase 'world literature' can be authoritatively used. It is only in the past couple of generations that 'world writing' has really ventured far beyond the European tradition, into writing from Africa or Native Australasia for example. It is a slow process, if a vigorous one.

A further question arising from Goethe's grand claims for world literature is whether what is true for literature is always true for poetry too, so that it is equally entitled to the claim of universality. Is poetry the best example of this? Generally speaking, grand claims for literature have tended to found their strongest warranty in poetry. In the late 1920s Paul Valéry, in the course of a discussion of 'Pure Poetry', said: 'To my mind, every written work, every product of language, contains certain fragments or recognizable elements endowed with properties...which I will provisionally call *poetic*.'

So, if poetry is entitled to make such claims to universality, what are they founded on? If there is something in all cultures that we might call poetry, what is the common factor that makes it so? Many attempts to find the definitive common element have been made, in the same way that they have for music. What is the poetry gene, we might ask—in the same way that structuralist literary theorists tried to find something they called *litterarité*, 'literariness', to qualify for categorization as literature? Mill insisted that we must go on looking for 'something peculiar in its nature', arguing that the fact that there is *felt* to be a difference

14

between poetry and other things must mean that there *is* such a difference. It is clear that it is not a matter of being written down. It has even been argued by some anthropologists that poetry in its metaphorical nature pre-dates all other uses of language, spoken as well as written. We will consider in Chapter 1 some of the suggestions that have been made as definitive factors.

Poetry and poetics

So it is obvious that very many approaches could have been taken in approaching poetry as a whole. This book is primarily concerned with what poetry is; it is not a handbook of the formal means it adopts to achieve its ends. Among the items in the 'Further Reading', the most valuable for my purposes, and the most comprehensive treatment of the whole area in English, is *The Princeton Encyclopedia of Poetry and Poetics* (the fourth edition was published in 2012). In attempting to define what has been thought indispensable to the definition of poetry across various ages and cultures we are starting with the theory, rather than the practice: a distinction between poetry and poetics which has been fundamental since the Greeks, and which we will constantly need to return to. This book aims to represent both theory and practice, and the relations between them, illustrating when possible by practice as well as theory. We must not underrate the importance of theory though and escape *too* readily into the refuge and indulgence of quotation: it was the examination of the idea of poetry, not its practice, which was said by Wallace Stevens to be 'one of the great subjects of study'. There is widespread justification for the distinction between poetry itself, and poetics as a more abstract consideration of the art of poetry, and for according poetics the same kind of centrality as poetry itself. In the Chinese, Japanese, and Indian traditions, discussions of poetics have been at least as prominent as in the West.

Notwithstanding the grand perspective on poetry and its discussion since the Greeks, the ambitious claims to universal application geographically and culturally, and the success of occasional anthologies of translations such as Mark Van Doren's *An Anthology of World Poetry*, most of this book is dependent on English illustration. One of the most quoted aphorisms about poetry is Robert Frost's definition that it is what fails to survive translation. This is a striking reservation, but it also suggests difficulties for any attempt to see the place and function of poetry in a wider context of world literature. No matter how we attempt to take into account the range of poetry across languages and eras, we can't escape very effectively the ethnocentricity that Goethe warns against. If it is important to work through to any extent the various categories in which poetry has been described and practised over millennia and cultures, then we will be heavily dependent on translators. And there are great translations that have crossed the divide to some extent, even if it remains impossible to represent other literatures with any fullness. Nobody who heard Ted Hughes read Lady Gregory's translation of the Irish folk-poem 'Donal Óg', something he did frequently at public readings, could maintain scepticism about the value and poetic quality of successful translations. And, just as there have been great eras of drama (in England the Elizabethan and Jacobean periods) and lyric (the early 19th century), so there have been great ages of translation: especially the 16th century when the works of classical and modern European literature were translated into English, producing classics of English that rank with any new imaginative works: Chapman's Homer (acknowledged by Keats—'Much have I travelled in the realms of gold'), Golding's Ovid, and Florio's Montaigne. In that period, it is ironic that Puttenham denies the name of 'very poet' to the translator 'who may well be said a versifier, but not a Poet'. The Loeb translations of the Victorian period and since, though they are often accused of being 'translatorese', often have a kind of majesty. C. Day-Lewis's Virgil and Robert Fitzgerald's versions of the Greek classics offer distinguished access to major foreign-language texts which are otherwise unavailable to readers without a reading knowledge of those languages. Some translations have a distinction which makes them major poetic works in their own right; in the current era, for example, translations of several poetic texts in various languages have been made impressively by the Northern Irish poet Ciaran Carson. And there are others: for various technological reasons ours may be another of the notable ages of translation. It is also a period in which interest in translation theory is on the increase.

There is one other related poetic phenomenon within world literature which might be mentioned finally—those few anthologies that have made a gallant attempt to represent world poetry, such as Van Doren's American *Anthology of World Poetry* dedicated 'To the Memory of John Dryden, Poet and Translator' and subtitled 'In English Translations by Chaucer, Swinburne, Dowson, Symons, Rossetti, Waley, Herrick, Pope, Francis Thompson and others.' The languages included—all in translation except the final three categories, English, Irish, and American—are Chinese, Japanese, Sanskrit, Arabian, Persian, Hebrew, Egyptian, Greek, Latin, Italian, Spanish, French, German, Scandinavian, and Russian. The range spreads across fifty-five centuries, and it is confined to lyric-length translations. There is no Homer therefore on grounds of length, and there is no Pindar because the editor 'discovered no English version of him which made him seem great—or even, for that matter, readable'. But the anthology is an impressive success within its confines, giving a better sense of the variety in world poetry than might have seemed possible. And it proposes rhythm as the crucial criterion, even in the translations, from Bashō to the Native American poems translated by Mary Austin, side by side with the canonical figures.

Van Doren says that he demanded pre-existent excellent verse translations in his 'anthology of the world's best poetry in the best English I could unearth, and when I found no good English at all I left the poet out'. Remarkably, his enterprise tends to restore our belief in poetry, whether we can rationalize it or not, and it anticipates impressively a phenomenon—short poetry in translation—which has become increasingly dominant over the following century, as indeed the question of translation as a whole has. But, while it does partially restore our belief in the breadth of poetry, it is unsettling to reflect that as recently as 1929 this cosmopolitan and wide-ranging *Anthology of World Poetry* had very few women writers and no writers of colour from the modern era. This caveat is necessary because, in an anthology that includes Sappho and begins with 200 pages of poems from Chinese, Japanese, Sanskrit, Arabian, Persian, Hebrew, and Egyptian, its 163 pages of poems in English, from Chaucer to Robert Graves, represents women by three short poems by Christina Rossetti and one by Alice Meynell. It seems to be the case that, before the later 20th century, the gender and racial bias in the canon was much more marked in the modern era than in the distant past.

Broadly speaking, my discussion of poetics has drawn on as much of the traditional discussion of the Western tradition as I know about, and as much of the Eastern tradition as slight exposure supplemented by a limited amount of active research could facilitate. For poetic texts I have used only English, because (though I can quote poems in Irish, and passages from Dante, and Latin) for the most part I only feel qualified to evaluate and wholly understand what is written in my birth language and, in some cases, translated into it. It is such a difficult matter to pronounce generally and to any useful effect on the nature of poetry that it seems wise in doing so at least to keep to the language that we can fully understand.

There are further inevitable biases in my discussion: not only towards the language I know best but towards the poets and critics I know and like best. There is a wealth of Irish examples, especially from Yeats and Heaney, and Robert Frost's poetics are recurrent here. There are some biases which are not my fault: the canon of poetry and its traditions are strongly skewed towards the male and the powerful in a way that is not easy to redress. In English it would be unrealistic to avoid Sidney or Shelley. But while conceding that there will be ways in which any discussion will not be universally representative of poetry in all cultures, there is something common to the function of poetry everywhere which means that a thoroughgoing analysis of it anywhere will help to establish its nature. I have been sustained throughout by a belief that there is after all something poetry does that nothing else can, and that this is something of major value in our world and time as in all others.

But we must be cautious too. If we make such grand claims as this for poetry we must be slow to confer the designation of poetry or poet. After all, to understand the distinction and skill of such writers as those I invoke at various points here—Dante or Donne or Catullus or Shakespeare—we must see it as something rare, before we claim that poetry is something of equal value in all eras. Everyone finds tiresome the claim that theirs is 'a great age of poetry'. As it happens, it might be felt that ours is not a great age of poetry for various reasons, mostly to do with the dominance of fictional forms like the novel or cinema, or the competitive energy of popular music; but that is not the point: this reservation is a generalization as pointless as the opposing claim. Still, we must be slow to claim greatness, in the same way that we are put on our guard by people who introduce themselves as a poet. We have to wait for the judgement of the ages and the corroboration of readers and critics; in fact, most ages have felt their own was a bad time for poetry: Crites, 'a person of sharp judgement', says in Dryden's *Essay of Dramatic Poesy* in 1667, 'There are so few who write well in this age that methinks any praises should be welcome.'

On the whole, although it is commonly said that the best criticism of poetry is made by critics who are themselves poets, the most insightful and disinterested criticism is often written by those who are solely critics: writers like Edmund Wilson, F. R. Leavis, Frank Kermode, Helen Vendler, and Christopher Ricks. But we must also be ready to recognize and acknowledge poetic greatness when we encounter it. Poetry is generally acknowledged to be important, but it can only be so if it works its way and makes a major impact or contribution. Of course, this contribution may be primarily to entertain, as Coleridge says; but if so it must be entertainment of a high and useful order if it is to warrant the lofty claims made by Sidney and Goethe and Brodsky, quoted at the start of this introduction.

The chapters of this short book attempt to deal with issues that the Introduction has raised briefly in relation to the universality of poetry. Chapter 1 considers some of the ways poetry has been defined and regarded over the ages, and the various things that have been proposed as indispensable to it. Chapter 2 considers the areas in which poetry seems to have particular authority and aptness: love, death, and nature, for example. Chapter 3 deals with the language of poetry, its special devices and effects—the things that constitute what used to be called 'style' and its relation to the question of correctness. Chapter 4 considers the genres of poetry—not just epic, dramatic, or lyric (Plato's categories) but other areas in which it wields authority or is salutary: in associating particular forms with such things as self-expression or representing a national spirit, for example. A genre of popular poetry is proposed there, as well as generic categories like elegy and poetry of consolation. Chapter 5 is concerned with poets and readers, and their respective roles in the creation of meaning—first, whether the term poet is reserved for a kind of elect or is a name anyone can aspire to. That chapter ends by considering the whole question of authorship and authority: whether the poem generally—or ever—speaks in the voice of the poet, and how that voice may relate to its audience. Also considered briefly in Chapter 5 is the function of critics and readers: a function which has attained increasing prominence in the 20th century and since, with the emergence of theories of reader response and the reception of poetry.

From this account of the chapters, it will be clear what this book is not: it is not a handbook of the details of poetic effects (many successful books of the kind exist and are noted in the 'Further Reading' section), with illustrations of such things as metrical or other formal poetic devices. Consideration of these will only occur where they are said to be definitive aspects of what poetry is and the forms in which it occurs, which is my abiding subject. And if the matter threatens to become impossibly divided and uncertain, we can be reassured by reflecting that all societies seem to have had something equivalent to what we call poetry and to have valued it highly. So our quest is worthwhile even if it is vagarious and inconclusive. That quest is at the heart of the values that determine what it is to be human: a quest that is, in Wallace Stevens's phrase, 'one of the enlargements of life'.

Chapter 1
Truths universally acknowledged

At the end of his lectures published as *The Use of Poetry and the Use of Criticism*, T. S. Eliot says, 'I have not attempted any definition of poetry, because I can think of none which does not assume that the reader knows what it is, or which does not falsify by leaving out much more than it can include.' This counsel of despair says that, as we have seen, there are no truths acknowledged universally about the nature and function of poetry; but some recurrent forceful views have been expressed on the matter. In identifying poets primarily as versifiers, Aristotle says, the public 'completely misses the point that the capacity to produce an imitation is the essential characteristic of the poet'. The idea that art is mimetic—that it reproduces something or imitates something—is primarily associated in the West with this observation in Aristotle's *Poetics*; but Plato too thought that poetry, like all art, was founded on imitation. The view that the poet is an originating, sensitive instrument that responds to nature is founded in this idea of imitation. Where the Greek philosophers diverged was in their views about what was being imitated. Aristotle said that art imitates nature itself, while Plato, and the Neoplatonists who were so influential in the later European tradition, believed that the importance of art was that it imitated the transcendental forms that precede and underlie the perceived world of nature. So in English, Coleridge's and Wordsworth's argument between the grand and simple was partly parallel to the very ancient opposition noted here, between what might in brief be called a transcendental and a naturalistic view of poetry. One way of placing Coleridge's high claims for the imagination is to see them in the transcendentalist Platonic tradition which had been firmly reinscribed in Western discussions by Renaissance Neoplatonism. And it is clear that the Platonic view of art and poetry makes possible very grand claims for those things, even if this was one of the views that led Plato himself to deplore the factual unreliability of poetry.

There are various points we could start at in deciding between definitions of poetry. A long-established argument is between two schools of belief about the nature of poetry and what it is for: whether its object is pleasure or something more practical—in Greek terms, hedonistic or utilitarian. Many of the opposing dualities that have been suggested correspond to these two: Horace's *dulce et utile*, 'pleasurable and practical'; Sidney's view that it must 'teach, move and delight'; Coleridge's view that poetry had for its immediate object 'pleasure, not truth'; Chaucer's *'solaas'* or *'sentence'* in *The Canterbury Tales*.

A spirited argument of the case for the pleasurable, non-utilitarian view was mounted by W. B. Stanford in his vigorous *Enemies of Poetry* in 1980. Stanford uses the term 'factualism' to describe the empirical or socially utilitarian view of poetry (a view which could be identified with the strictures of the Elizabethan Puritans), seeing it as a betrayal of what poetry is in its essence. He argues for 'creative literature for its own sake'; again following Aristotle, he is asserting 'the uniqueness and autonomy of poetry'. In the Western tradition this fundamental argument recurs from Aristotle to the Formalists and Structuralists of the early 20th century, and on to writers like W. H. Auden: those who believe that poetry is a distinctive world with its own jurisdiction, against those (recalling the hostile commentators of the late 16th century) dubbed 'Enemies of Poetry' by Stanford—Plato, Richard Bentley in the 18th century, Jeremy Bentham, and the infamous purifier

Thomas Bowdler in the 19th, who all felt that poetry must be called to order and corrected by standards of history or morality. Stanford's main quarrel was with the classical scholars who evaluated Homer on grounds of historical plausibility rather than poetic inspiration, and with the anthropologists of the school of James Frazer in *The Golden Bough* who dismissed myths, including poetic myths, as 'mistaken explorations of phenomena...founded on ignorance and misapprehension'.

The medievalist Talbot Donaldson disapproved of his colleague D. W. Robertson's allegorical religious reading of the poem 'Maiden in the Moor Lay' for failing to show that the poem made any more sense 'as a poem' after his allegorical reading (identifying the 'Maiden' of this cryptic little anonymous poem as the Virgin Mary) than before it. This corrective is dogmatic in its assumption of the autonomy of poetry. The argument was pursued in the later 20th century by poets like Seamus Heaney in the title essay of his book *The Government of the Tongue*, where he says that part of what he means by that title is 'poetry as its own vindicating force'. It is an interesting phrase because, while it clearly declares a belief in poetry's autonomy, the word 'vindicating' has an undertone of responsibility in it which links to the more moral, public view. We raised in the Introduction the rights and wrongs of poetry's moral and social responsibilities; next we must explore some of the features that have been proposed, rightly or wrongly, as indispensable to poetry, starting with formal definitions such as rhyme, metre, and kinds of language (verse as opposed to prose, for example), and go on to consider some of the areas—love and nature for instance—where poetry has been thought to have particular authority or aptness, and attempting to draw some conclusions about poetry's special spheres of influence.

Must poetry always be in verse form?

Having accepted that what poetry, like the other arts, *does* is imitation, whether it is of nature or of something else, we might

go on to seek a definition of what poetry *is*, returning to the one
that has had the widest currency in English noted at the start
of the Introduction: sense 2a in the *OED* which stresses the idea
of pattern (using the word and its derivative twice in a brief
definition) that we will see is fundamental in both requirements
of sound (rhythm) and ritual as definitive qualities:

> 2a. The art or work of a poet. a. Composition in verse or some
> comparable patterned arrangement of language in which the
> expression of feelings and ideas is given intensity by the use of
> distinctive style and rhythm; the art of such a composition.
>
> Traditionally associated with explicit formal departure from the
> patterns of ordinary speech or prose, e.g. in the use of elevated
> diction, figurative language, and syntactical reordering.

In the senses covered here, everyone knows what poetry is. It is
a kind of literature that uses special linguistic devices of
organization and expression for aesthetic effect. In the crudest
formulation in English, it used to be said that poetry must 'rhyme,
scan and make sense'. This kind of 'commonsensical' meaning
(it has also been called 'empirical' and 'pragmatic') was dominant
in the 18th century, for example, when Hurd named versification
as the third of his three elements of poetry. This—rhyme, metre,
and so on in English—is considered in Chapter 3 on poetic
language and style. By this definition poetry is a matter of craft or
technique; these skills can be learned (and perhaps taught: a matter
of some contention in the current era of creative writing courses,
though it has usually been believed that some people—who are
therefore called 'poets'—develop them more readily than others,
as discussed in Chapter 5). This assumption, that the poetic art
is an innate skill belonging to only a minority of people—a kind
of priestly caste—was recently questioned, though not wholly
contradicted, by Simic who wonders, 'is poetry a state of mind
anyone may have from time to time or a gift only a rare few are
blessed with?' This understanding of poetry as the verbal activity

of a gifted craftsperson with particular skills, rather than a universal potential capacity, has a long heritage, and there have been periods—like the 18th century—when it was the generally accepted European view. Clearly, if we could narrow poetry down to a particular set of skills and techniques, it would be reasonable to argue that some people—'poets'—possess them to a degree beyond the ordinary, in the same way that some individuals are better musical performers or practitioners of sport. Whether those skills can similarly be improved with training and practice is the question at stake in discussions of creative writing teaching. Whether poetry is to be seen as divinely inspired, as argued by Puttenham, is another matter, and we will return to this in the next section.

There has been more or less universal agreement throughout the history of poetic analysis that the view that verse form is the essence of poetry is hopelessly reductive, for all its definitive convenience. In his *Apologie for Poetry*, the most authoritative and appealing of the English offshoots of Renaissance Italian discussions, Sidney acknowledges the common preference among poets for writing in verse, but still declares firmly that verse is 'but an ornament and no cause to Poetry, since there have been many most excellent poets that never versified, and now swarm many versifiers that need never answer to the name of poets', adding that 'David's Psalms are a divine poem', though written in a kind of prose, and that Heliodorus and Xenophon wrote poetical works of the greatest excellence about love and war: 'yet both writ in prose'. The great libertarian John Stuart Mill puts it more trenchantly, saying that the 'vulgarest answer' to the question 'What is Poetry?' is to 'confound it with metrical composition'. Even Heaney, with his belief in the vindicating power of poetry, says 'Joyce qualifies as a poet more than most writers of verse'. In the early 19th century, Coleridge says the same thing in *Biographia Literaria*, typifying the European Romantic view that reacted against the practical 18th-century definitions, in declaring that the prose of *Isaiah* chapter 1 'is poetry in the most emphatic sense', more so than the instructive verse of jingles like 'Thirty days hath September | April, June, and November'. The prose of Plato, for all his declared suspicions of poetry, has often been described as poetry, in recognition of what Coleridge (acknowledged by Wallace Stevens) called his 'dear, gorgeous nonsense'. And though, as we have said, Coleridge and his friend Wordsworth argued about the status of language within poetry—whether it should be grand or simple—Wordsworth took the same view of the inadequacy of verse form as a definitive quality, requiring in poems like 'Tintern Abbey' some more profound internal motivation in poetry. In the 4th century BC, Aristotle had declared the limitations of this commonsensical definition of poetry as metrical writing: 'The public classifies all those who write in metre as poets'; but he, like Sidney, Coleridge, and Mill, immediately proceeds to declare this classification ill-founded.

It is not only in the European tradition that such exclusively formalist verse-based definitions of poetry have been debated, whether credited or not. For example, in contrasting what poetry means in Chinese with what it means in English, Raymond Dawson takes the opposite, anti-elitist view, proposing 'not to bother with the sort of value-judgement that bestows this term [poetry] as an award of merit on certain kinds of verse of which it approves, but to use "poetry" as the name of all verse literature, leaving to others the task of defining what literature is'. This is ignoring the principal definitive issue, satisfied with a broadness of definition that has found favour with very few of the Western authorities from the Greeks to the present day; but it is salutary to be reminded that there are traditions that define poetry in purely formal terms in this way. It is a feature of written art in the Eastern tradition not shared with the Western: the word *seohwa* in Korean (adopted as a trademark by a Communications Company) is translated as 'writing and painting'. Painters made works in which poetry, calligraphy, and painting were combined to compose perfect artistic wholes. Calligraphic pictures are common features of decoration in Chinese households; calligraphy as artwork, as practised by David Jones or Christopher Isherwood, is rare in the European tradition. 'Concrete poetry'—shaping poems on the page, as composed by George Herbert or Dylan Thomas, is unusual in English. But of course verse form and other matters of craft and technique—the tricks of the trade—are of vital interest for poetry. Even if, as Coleridge and Sidney say, they are not definitive, they are a large part of what we expect when we read poetry nowadays. And we must not be too dismissive of the part played by metrical forms: as Dryden says in 'An Essay of Dramatic Poesy', we must 'make our Rime so properly a part of the Verse, that it should never mislead the sense, but itself be led and governed by it'.

Furthermore, in declaring metrical form not to be definitive, we must not underestimate the place of sound in poetry. As with music, some connection of poetry with sound is often proposed as an indispensable quality. Aristotle says in the *Poetics* that poetry has two causes; the first is imitation, but 'next, there is the instinct for harmony and rhythm, metres being manifestly sections of rhythm'. Music cannot be called music if it is not expressed in some sonic medium; in the same way poetry has to have some kind of rhythmic structure to be called poetry. It is notable how even commentators who have taken very different views of poetry—as formal or conceptual; abstract or practical; pure or applied—have mostly begun by declaring the element of sound to be indispensable, whether it is consciously realized or not. The commonest word in English for this definitive quality is the inexact, but essential, term 'rhythm' (which links to 'patterning' in the *OED* definition: now patterning in sound rather than in sense or other formal recurrences). I am not yet emphasizing enough the importance of sound as a feature of poetry; it is discussed in the section 'The sound of sense' in Chapter 3. And, in dismissing metrical forms as universal requirements of poetry, we should still note the usefulness of rhyme as an aid to memory in poetry. The value of 'learning by heart' (or 'by rote') is emphasized by writers such as Ted Hughes, and there is no doubt that the clinching echo of rhyme aids the memory. This can be a weakness as well as a strength: Alexander Pope, in his prodigious 'Essay on Criticism' (written when he was twenty), mocks the predictability of rhyme as well as poetic diction:

> Where-e'er you find the cooling Western Breeze,
> In the next Line, it whispers thro' the Trees;
> If Chrystal Streams with pleasing Murmurs creep,
> The reader's threaten'd (not in vain) with Sleep.

But in spite of this warning, Pope was himself one of the greatest and most dedicated exponents of rhyme in the English language. His success with it, like that of other virtuosi like Byron, proves its worth.

Ritual and tradition as requirements?

Pope was doubtful too about the tendency to identify poetry with its formal qualities generally:

> But most by numbers judge a Poet's Song,
> And smooth or rough, with them, is right or wrong;
> In the bright Muse tho' thousand Charms conspire,
> Her voice is all these tuneful Fools admire,
> Who haunt Parnassus but to please their Ear,
> Not mend their Minds, as some to Church repair,
> Not for the Doctrine, but the Musick there.

So, if verse form and tunefulness is mostly agreed not to be essential for the definition of poetry, to which of the Muse's Charms might we turn instead? A feature which is frequently proposed as indispensable to poetry is some connexion with ritual: T. S. Eliot declared emphatically that '*All* art emulates the condition of ritual. That is what it comes from and to that it must always return for nourishment.' This is recognizing the fundamental social origins of poetry which are part of what warrants its claim to universal significance. In one of the most interesting discussions of the nature of poetry from Eliot's period, *Illusion and Reality* (1937), Christopher Caudwell argued that ethnological research in various cultures has shown that heightened language—a special 'register', as it is sometimes called—has emerged universally from the significant social circumstances in which language was used—magic spells, religious chants, and weather prayers—and that this might be thought to be the original motivation for poetry.

Certainly, such hieratic, religion-linked definitions are recurrent in all ages: Sidney reminds us that among the Romans 'a poet was called *vates*, which is as much as a deviner, foreseer, or prophet': a 'heavenly title'. Indeed this identification preceded the Romans: in Plato's *Ion* dialogue, Socrates says (partly with scepticism) the poets compose, not by reason, but 'from the impulse of divinity within them'. The heavenly title is appropriate, because, to quote Sidney's example again, such things as 'the holy David's Psalms are a divine poem'. We might note in passing that both things make significant use of the mnemonic usefulness of metrical repetition and rhyme; priestly castes and poets both find liturgical patterning valuable for performance.

Such claims as Eliot's have appeal because ritual seems to be common to all cultures—to be culture's most definitive idea, indeed. Ritual—with its associations of repeated pattern that it shares with the notion of rhythm—might also seem to be as near as we can get to the *formal* essence of poetry, the verbal art which seems most dependent on the ritualistic. Ritual, one might say, is the connective system between a culture and the formal art that celebrates or expresses it. In Eliot's time, Paul Valéry said something similar in *The Art of Poetry*: 'It must not be forgotten that for centuries poetry was used for purposes of enchantment'. And it is of course significant that the touchstone line from Dante chosen by Arnold and Eliot is Piccarda's declaration of religious peace (quoted at the beginning of this book's Introduction).

In dividing up responsibility for the different aspects of poetry in the *Lyrical Ballads*, Wordsworth and Coleridge took due account of the varying demands of the worldly and the transcendental. They said that two sorts of poem might be taken to represent these 'cardinal points of poetry': one in which 'the incidents and agents were to be, in part at least, supernatural'; the second in which 'subjects were to be chosen from ordinary life'. 'Poetry has either the power of exciting the sympathy of the reader by a faithful adherence to the truth of nature, or the power of giving the interest of novelty by the modifying colours of imagination.' In the division of labour, the ritualistic aspects of poetry were assigned to Coleridge who would deal with the second kind, drawing, as with Valéry's 'enchantment', on the 'colours of imagination'—hence 'The Rime of the Ancient Mariner' (see Figure 1); Wordsworth would provide the poems of ordinary life, faithfully representing 'characters and incidents...such as will be found in every village and its vicinity where there is a meditative and feeling mind to seek after them'. In this we readily recognize the Coleridge–Wordsworth opposition as it is generally understood: 'the shaping spirit of imagination' of Coleridge's great 'Dejection' ode, as against the writing of 'a man speaking to men' of Wordsworth's *Preface*. And we see too the affinities of Coleridge's emphasis with Eliot's argument for ritual as the essence of art.

Linked to ritual is the widely found idea of inspiration, by either a divinity or an irresistibly motivating person or experience, according to which poets are not just makers from their own resources but responsive instruments, in Matthew Arnold's words, 'waiting for the spark from heaven to fall'. The poet is inspired by a Muse, as by a divinity. This is a restatement of the Platonic idea of poetry as transcendent; one of its most dramatic and effective expressions in English comes in Coleridge's 'Kubla Khan' with its 'deep romantic chasm...holy and enchanted'. The poem ends (insofar as it does end) with an imagined picture of the inspired or frenzied artist in that Romantic environment of icy caves and sunny dome:

1. Gustave Doré, illustration to Coleridge's 'The Rime of the Ancient Mariner', 1877.

I would build that dome in air,
That sunny dome! those caves of ice!
And all who heard should see them there
And all should cry Beware! Beware!
His flashing eyes, his floating hair!
Weave a circle round him thrice

32

> And close your eyes with holy dread.
> For he on honey-dew hath fed
> And drunk the milk of Paradise.

This inspired and frenzied figure is an extreme example of the Romantic artist whose inspiration is the 'milk of Paradise' rather than any internal impulse towards making and composition. Poetic inspiration is something that comes from outside the poet. And of course this characterization of the poet does not begin with the Romantics—Coleridge's artist here recalls Theseus's poet in *A Midsummer Night's Dream*:

> The poet's eye, in a fine frenzy rolling,
> Doth glance from heaven to earth, from earth to heaven;
> And as imagination bodies forth
> The forms of things unknown, the poet's pen
> Turns them to shapes, and gives to aery nothing
> A local habitation and a name.

This links to the idea of the Muse, as someone or something that prompts the production of art through a kind of mystical inspiration; we recognize an affinity with the Sibyl of Cumae in Book 6 of Virgil's *Aeneid* who 'chants wildly in the cave, trying to shake off the god from her breast: all the more he tires her raging mouth'. The Romantics are reverting in an extreme way to a Platonic, transcendental view of poetry as something beyond nature and reason. Clearly the Muse is a figure of the supernatural in the same way as the numinous, divinely inspired Sibyl is. The trouble is, as again Socrates slyly suggests, that it is the poets themselves who tell us that 'the poets have this peculiar ministration in the world'.

In the post-Romantic era, poetry—or art in general—has increasingly been seen as an alternative to ritual or religion, rather than a component or instance of it. Nietzsche famously saw art as a replacement for religion, saying 'Art raises its head where Creeds relax'. In the words of Anthony Storr, Nietzsche declared that 'for many people, the concert hall and the art gallery have replaced the church as places where the "divine" can be encountered'. This was particularly beautifully put by Wallace Stevens in 'The Man with the Blue Guitar':

> Exceeding music must take the place
> Of empty heaven and its hymns.

The link of ritual with sound, mentioned briefly at the end of the previous section, is crucial; it is indeed 'Exceeding music' that takes 'the place | Of empty heaven and its hymns', in poetry as well as religion. If heaven is empty, the 'exceeding music' must be composed by some more calculated, earthly agency and have its own rituals. But, like other more obviously selective views of poetry, the religion-related definition turns out to be limited in its application. We are told that there is no religious poetry at all in Chinese (though once again we would have to check the cultural translation of our terms; after all, one of Confucius's inferences from *The Book of Poetry* prescribes 'Let yourself be inspired by *Poetry*, confirmed by ritual, and perfected by music'). And there are modern views of poetry for which the notion of the Muse and supernatural inspiration of any kind are not only unfashionable but irrelevant.

However, even if poetry does not have to be an expression of the tenets of any religion, some ritualistic connection with social expression from its oral origins seems to have survived to its most wholly textual developments. In the same period as Eliot and Valéry, Lascelles Abercrombie combined the ritual with the sonic in his definition of 'Great' (as opposed to 'Pure') poetry: 'I will call it, compendiously, "incantation", the power of using words so as to produce in us a sort of enchantment.' The word 'incantation' makes the link between sound and ritual observance perfectly, and it describes what it is in our modern response to poetry that connects with its original socially ritualistic operation. Seamus

Heaney's early poem 'The Diviner' uses the rural water-diviner as an image to link the agricultural and the artistic.

> Cut from the green hedge a forked hazel-stick
> That he held tight by the arms of the V;
> Circling the terrain, hunting the pluck
> Of water, nervous, but professionally
>
> Unfussed. The pluck came sharp as a sting.
> The rod jerked down with precise convulsions,
> Spring water suddenly broadcasting
> Through a green aerial its secret stations.
>
> The bystanders would ask to have a try.
> He handed them the rod without a word.
> It lay dead in their grasp till nonchalantly
> He gripped expectant wrists. The hazel stirred.

This poem combines a remarkable number of the ritualistic associations of poetry from its title onwards: the social ritual often claimed for poetry's origins; the scepticism that it prompts in the rational intelligence; the mystery of its transmission. As a figure for the notion of transmission, Socrates in the *Ion* describes how the Muse operates like a magnet which not only attracts iron rings itself but transmits to them the power of exercising such attraction in turn, and, 'communicating through those whom she has first inspired to all others capable of that first enthusiasm, creates a chain and a succession'. Similarly the Muse—like the water-diviner here—is 'communicating through those whom she has first inspired', creating a chain and a succession to be followed by acolytes.

Another important idea shared by religion and literature is tradition, something which is also active in the passing on of local skills. The history of all religions is concerned to define and observe the tenets that are essential to them. Traditional practice is the guardian of this history. One of the most celebrated discussions of literary history in English is T. S. Eliot's essay 'Tradition and the Individual Talent', which views all literary practice as an addition to the pre-existing literary tradition as a whole. An idea like 'biblical tradition' in English has much in common with the phrase 'literary tradition' which it influences. This is not only a critic's perspective: the writer in a particular form is aware of previous practitioners in what constitutes a tradition, just as the religious minister is repeating a received liturgy.

Different terms have been used to describe these literary relationships in different eras: in the 20th century, the rather elaborate term 'intertextuality' was developed to describe the order of literary works. Earlier the term 'literary allusion' was used to refer to how writers (poets in particular) signalled their connections with earlier practitioners and themes. For example, it would be a limitation in reading English poetry not to see the awareness of Shakespeare or Spenser in a writer like Keats. This allusiveness is found widely across poetic tradition; Chinese poetry, like Skaldic verse's kennings in Old Norse, requires knowledge of other stories, myths, legends, and settings to be intelligible. From the reader's perspective, as well as the writer's, a sense of the tradition in which a poet is writing is important. To take a famous example, to understand the impact of the opening of Eliot's *The Waste Land*—'April is the cruellest month | Breeding lilacs out of the dead land'—we need to link it by contrast to the idyllic opening of Chaucer's *Canterbury Tales*:

Whan that Aprill with his shoures soote	*gentle showers*
The droghte of Marche hath perced to the roote	*dryness, pierced.*

There is a tradition of such spring-opening poems—*reverdie* in medieval French—which both Chaucer and Eliot are operating with. Eliot's 'Tradition and the Individual Talent' is recognizing that the 'talent' of the new writer has to be seen in the context of a preceding literary 'tradition' among which the new work takes its place, giving rise to a new order in the works within the tradition. For the new writer the wording of the earlier constitutes a kind of liturgy.

Metaphor and the figurative

Robert Frost said in *The Atlantic Monthly* in 1946: 'There are many other things I have found myself saying about poetry, but the chiefest of these is that it is metaphor, saying one thing and meaning another, saying one thing in terms of another, the pleasure of ulteriority.' In saying that poetry had 'traditionally' been associated with departures from normal language, the *OED*'s definition (see p. 26) proposed three linguistic ways in which these departures take place: 'elevated diction, figurative language, and syntactical reordering'. Of those three essential linguistic areas, we will briefly consider the importance of syntax in poetry in English in Chapter 3; stylistic contrast by elevated or plain diction is for historical reasons very important in English, and this is discussed in some detail in Chapter 2. But figurativeness—what Frost calls 'metaphor'—seems to be central to the practice of poetry in all languages. Aristotle's requirements of poetic language are strikingly in key with the *OED*'s definitions; immediately after recognizing the departures from the norms of language, Aristotle in *The Poetics* turns to extol metaphor and figurative language: 'By deviating in exceptional cases from the normal idiom, the language will gain distinction; while, at the same time, the partial conformity with usage will give perspicuity.' But, like Frost, he concludes: 'the greatest thing by far is to have a command of metaphor'.

Poetics is particularly concerned with the way that poetry foregrounds the figurative and metaphorical activity in language. In the 14th century Boccaccio said that it is impossible to tell a story from which some moral inference cannot be drawn; similarly all language use involves some figurative relation to its literal underlay. In one of the most suggestive guides to English verse, *Rhyme's Reason*, John Hollander acknowledges Frost: 'Good verse of any sort is nevertheless only half the story of good poetry, whose essential character is what Wallace Stevens calls "fictive", and Robert Frost "ulterior", or "saying one thing and meaning another", or what we could simply call not being literal.'

It is not immediately obvious why this should be the case; why has it been thought more effective to describe things in terms other than the simply literal? Figurative language was the first requirement even in Hurd's 'pragmatic' 18th-century definition of poetry; the second was that poetry is a 'fiction'. Using metaphor, or statement in indirect terms based on resemblance rather than identity, means that the poet can't be accused of lying by direct statement. As we have heard, Sidney said famously that 'the poet nothing affirmes, and therefore never lyeth. For, as I take it, to lye is to affirme that to be true which is false.' This ingenious view of poetic language as fictional, if not downright mendacious, was the deviousness given as one of the reasons for poetry's banishment from Plato's *Republic*.

But, for whatever reason, poetry seems always to have chosen to use linguistic means to 'say one thing in terms of another', as Frost says, and not simply to 'say what happened' in literal terms. Aristotle defined the making of good metaphors as involving 'an eye for resemblances'. In the Western Christian tradition, Thomas Aquinas follows St Augustine in seeing the felicity of figurative expression, though he declares the priority of the literal sense, even in theology.

Dante in the *Convivio* accepts the dominance of the literal sense, but goes on to propose a figurative interpretation of it—for example in his gloss on Ovid's account of Orpheus: 'As when Ovid says that Orpheus with his lyre made wild beasts tame and made trees and rocks approach him; which would say that the wise man with the instrument of his voice makes cruel hearts tender and humble, and moves to his will such as have not the life of science and of art; for they that have not the rational life are as good as stones.'

Providing figurative interpretation was the principal means by which Christian writers of the Middle Ages justified the study of pagan classical texts. The justification did not always go unchallenged; Tertullian, a Christian writer from Carthage, in his work *Prescription Against Heretics* (early 3rd century), asked, 'What has Athens to do with Jerusalem?' Why do Church writers read and expound the secular classics of Greece and Rome? This can be seen as an early version of the argument between public responsibility and artistic licence which has occurred throughout the history of poetics. The theologian Alcuin of York adapted Tertullian's question to ask why Christian poets turned aside to write—or read—about Germanic figures like Ingeld (who occurs in *Beowulf*): 'Quid Hinieldus cum Christo?'—'What has Ingeld to do with Christ?'

Despite these concerns—and perhaps partly in answer to them—a great deal of the literary ingenuity of the principal literary writers of medieval Europe was devoted to making the connection between the classics and contemporary poetry: works such as Dante's *Convivio* and his 'Letter to Cangrande', which traced four levels of meaning in texts, derived from the fundamental opposition between the literal and the figurative. Justification for the opposition could be found in St Paul's Second Letter to the Corinthians: 'the letter killeth, but the spirit giveth life'. The ingenuity of Western literary criticism was founded on making figurative links between the Old and the New Testament: seeing, for example, the sacrifice of Isaac by Abraham as a prefiguring of the sacrifice of Christ on Calvary. This indebtedness was recognized by literary critics like Northrop Frye in his study of Biblical figuration, *The Great Code*.

But such matters of interpretation can't be the only, or even the principal reason for the use of figuration in poetry. Figurative expression is central to the whole operation of language; many of

39

our commonest words are entrenched, worn-out metaphors, the metaphoric drift of which has been lost sight of. For example, in the phrase 'the present state of affairs', the main words contain three submerged verbs: *sentire* (to think); *stare* (to stand); and *facere* (to do). But the metaphorical application has become totally dominant. Some poets, notably W. H. Auden, saw it to be an important part of the poet's job to bring back to the surface the etymological senses that had been submerged and worn away through general usage. When Adam in *Paradise Lost* compliments Eve on being 'elegant and exact of taste', by 'elegant' he means she is capable of choosing well (from Latin *eligere*, to choose). This hendiadys, the figure which uses two terms to convey a single meaning, now reads like a pair of unrelated compliments.

Various terms have been devised to describe the relationship between the literal image and the figurative meaning it connotes. The most influential 20th-century pairing in English was 'tenor' (the underlying sense) and 'vehicle' (the image that carried that sense), first devised by I. A. Richards and applied to literary analysis. The dominant pairing for language in general, translated from the French of Ferdinand de Saussure, was 'signifier' and 'signified'. In an intellectual sense the tenor—the signified—is the more important; the implication is that, once the vehicle has done its signifying work, it can disappear. It has been said that what distinguishes literary language from everyday usage is precisely the fact that it does not disappear once it has been understood: that is, the signifier is at least as important as the signified. In a poetic context (as Augustine says and as Dante deduces from Ovid) the actual words are always of primary importance, pleasing in their own terms (Donaldson would say 'as a poem'). One of Shakespeare's most admired and popular sonnets begins:

> That time of year thou may'st in me behold
> When yellow leaves, or none, or few, do hang
> Upon those boughs which shake against the cold,
> Bare ruin'd choirs, where late the sweet birds sang.

The metaphor that develops the comparison between the ageing and decaying of the speaker and the movement of the year towards winter is sustained through the poem, following the opening with a variation on the same metaphorical theme.

> In me thou see'st the twilight of such day
> As after sunset fadeth in the west;
> Which by and by black night doth take away,
> Death's second self , that seals up all in rest.

Shakespeare's language at its most powerful has a marked tendency towards the metaphorical: the most wounding thing Antony says to Cleopatra when they quarrel is 'I found you as a morsel cold | Upon dead Caesar's trencher'.

The traditional teaching term to describe the devices that convert the literal to the figurative used to be 'figures of speech', a formula that recognized the origins of the poetic in the speech of spoken contexts, such as religious preaching, or the law, or drama. Of crucial importance here is rhetoric, the devices of persuasion. W. B. Yeats said, 'We make out of the quarrel with others, rhetoric, but of the quarrel with ourselves, poetry.' This opposition makes a good aphorism (derived, he tells us, from a half-remembered observation made by his father in a letter); but poetry and rhetoric are often inextricably in collaboration. It has often been observed that the work of Aristotle which has most to say about modern conceptions of poetry with their predilection for the lyric is not the *Poetics* with its primary concern for drama, but the *Rhetoric*. We might claim that, if the medium of poetic ritual is sound, it seems equally indisputable that its method is something like rhetoric, the art of persuasion and the special effects used in the making of poetry which help it to achieve its impact, regardless of truth. These persuasive effects are not merely such things as rhyme and metre (clearly connected with sound), but also those 'figures of speech' which may be features of sound, such as alliteration, or may be devices which serve to persuade rationally or intellectually, often through metaphor. It is often observed that the impetus for the creation of classifications of literary effects—guides to figures of speech and tropes—was the codification of the practice of Homer. If poets want to achieve an effective practice, they should do as Homer does.

But of course when Yeats contrasted poetry with rhetoric, saying that it is 'out of the quarrel with ourselves we make poetry', he was claiming that poetry is the most intense form of self-expression. This view internalizes the art of poetry, which might be thought to narrow its range and effectiveness. By contrasting poetry with rhetoric as what we make out of the quarrel with others, Yeats's own quarrel in the context is with Shelley's famous claim that the poets are the unacknowledged legislators, the subject of Chapter 2.

In the Western tradition the rhetorical devices for persuasion were recognized and categorized from Aristotle onwards; the text that was most influential in Europe was a work of about 100 AD called *On the Sublime* written by Longinus, about whom nothing is known. But for literature an equally significant moment in the West was the reorganization of rhetoric by the French humanist Petrus Ramus in the 16th century, according to which the organizing structural divisions of rhetoric (invention—the finding of the linguistic materials; and disposition—the ordering of them) were assigned to logic, so that literary rhetoric became purely a matter of style (*elocutio*) which had been the third division of rhetoric according to classical authorities. This has had a major impact on the discussion of poetry since the Renaissance when 'style' in various senses has certainly been seen as the indispensable feature of poetry's language. Even before Ramus though, the connection of rhetoric with poetry was close: the early 15th-century London poet, Thomas Hoccleve, referred to 'My maister Chaucer, flour of rethours all', where the word 'rethour'—practitioner of rhetoric—means poet.

We are taken back, yet again, to Aristotle and his view that no matter or subject can be divorced from the form in which it is expressed, a doctrine which made a reappearance in the discussions of style in the earlier 20th century when it was proposed that it was not possible to talk about the meaning of a poem at all without reference to the form, or style, in which it was expressed. There were several familiar versions of this principle, of which perhaps the most famous was Marshall McLuhan's 'The medium is the message', much re-employed. Within poetics, the term style has gained a new usefulness within linguistics, having its own branch of 'stylistics' which is primarily concerned with the language of poetry, seen as a well that the individual poem can draw from, rather than the characteristic practice that makes a particular writer identifiable. In the heyday of what was called 'new criticism' in the earlier 20th century, the text of the poem was declared to be the only evidence that the critic should be concerned with. The words on the page had all authority; nothing in the context beyond them—such as the circumstances of their production and the poet's life history—was to the point. We will return to this in Chapter 5, in consideration of the presence—or not—of the poet in the poem.

Chapter 2
Poetry's areas of authority and application

Having considered what poetry has been said to be, we might turn next to examine where it has been thought to have most authority and where it lacks it. In the course of his insistence that in the modern era lyric is the dominant genre in poetry, rather than Aristotle's epic or drama (something discussed in Chapter 4), as its opposite Wordsworth replaced history, which Sidney had declared the logical opposite of poetry, with what he called 'matter of fact, or science'. But such grand oppositions have never gone unchallenged. Coleridge defines a poem as pleasure–seeking of its nature, and Wordsworth makes poetry a worthy adversary for science: the limitations of both views were witheringly pilloried by Thomas Love Peacock in 'The Four Ages of Poetry' (1818) as settling for 'gewgaws and rattles for the grown babies of the age … as if there were no such things in existence as mathematicians, astronomers, chemists, moralists, metaphysicians, historians, politicians, and political economists'. This is not only opposing one view of poetry to another; it is seeing poetry as less important than the disciplines Peacock lists, the discussions of which are normally conducted in prose.

However, in the 19th century, as in other eras, similarities between poetry and scientific disciplines were also claimed, especially with reference to the idea of 'beauty' in mathematics and its relation to poetic form. The Irish mathematician William Rowan Hamilton warned us not to be

> surprised that there should exist an analogy, and that not faint nor distant, between the workings of the poetical and the scientific imagination...With all the real differences between Poetry and Science, there exists, notwithstanding, a strong resemblance between them; in the power which both possess to lift the mind beyond the stir of earth...in the enthusiasm which both can inspire, and the fond aspirations after fame which both have a tendency to enkindle; in the magic by which each can transport her votaries into a world of her own creating.

Newton's *Principia* he saw partly 'as a structure of beautiful thoughts'. The modern mathematician Roger Penrose believes that mathematics is not just a set of elegant mental operations but a series of truths which are already 'there' (such as that 317 is a prime number)—'truths whose existence is quite independent of the mathematicians' activities'. Penrose calls this idea 'mathematical Platonism', making for it the same claims of access to truth as exalted views of poetry make. The same view of the underlying symmetry of art and physics is taken by Murray Gell-Mann in 'Beauty, Truth and Physics', and by the mathematician Marcus de Sautoy.

But poetry and science have been more commonly seen as opposites. Coleridge called poetry 'that species of composition which is opposed to works of science', rejecting its most familiar formal oppositional pairing, with prose, the usual medium of the more serious, scientific discourses listed by Peacock. In his 'Observations Prefixed to *Lyrical Ballads*' in 1800 Coleridge says that it is against his 'own judgment' that he uses '"Poetry"...as opposed to the word Prose, and synonymous with metrical composition.' Poetry, he says, is not opposed to prose, which is the alternative to verse as a form of the organization of writing: 'the only strict antithesis to Prose is Metre'. Wordsworth too was reluctant to oppose poetry to prose, preferring to contrast it to science as the discourse for which prose was most natural. In 'English Bards and Scotch Reviewers', Byron rudely pilloried this pronouncement of Wordsworth

> Who, both by precept and example, shows
> That prose is verse, and verse is merely prose.

Nevertheless, the contrast between poetry and prose is a fundamental categorical distinction, primarily with application to written forms. (Since Molière, it has been debated whether the term prose can be applied to non-written language. Is it really prose that M. Jourdain is speaking in *Le Bourgeois Gentilhomme*?) The poetry–prose distinction might seem to be a matter of possession, or not, of the poetic formalities considered here (and in Chapter 3): but we have seen that it has generally been agreed that some prose—like that of the Authorized Version of the Bible—may claim the standing of the poetic at least as much as routine versifying.

A different way of approaching the poetry–prose opposition might be to consider the matter of generalization. It has often been said that generalization is the strength of poetry while prose, especially in fiction, keeps to the particular. This raises problems of course: Blake said 'To particularize is the Alone Distinction of Merit'. But the heritage of general truth is a distinguished one in poetry, from the Old Testament Proverbs, to Old English wisdom poetry, to Blake himself in his 'Proverbs of Hell' and 'Auguries of Innocence' (discussed in Chapter 4). In vernacular usage, we recognize a difference between what is 'prosaic' and what is 'sheer poetry', whether with reference to verse or prose. The situation in Chinese is even more complicated, where the term for poetry, *shih*, excludes large sections of verse literature, and where it is dubious whether the term 'prose' is meaningful at all.

Another, more tempting prose–poetry opposition is made in a celebrated poem by Emily Dickinson:

> I dwell in Possibility—
> A fairer House than Prose—
> More numerous of Windows—
> Superior—for Doors—

The imaginative reach of poetry (which is what 'Possibility' is usually thought to refer to here) is unrestricted. If politics is the art of the possible, poetry extends its imaginative coverage to what is not confined to the practically possible. It has often been claimed that poetry is an earlier occurrence in cultures, and that prose—a written form corresponding to discursive speech, rejecting the embellishments employed by poetry—is a more mannered and, in a temporal sense, a more advanced development. In the medieval courts of Charlemagne and King Alfred, for example, the creation of a vernacular written prose to express matters that were discussed in Latin prose can be seen as an earlier Renaissance. But despite the practicality of prose, and its various claims to artistry in such writers as Sir Thomas Browne, Jonathan Swift, Samuel Johnson, Jane Austen, and Henry James, the social priority of poetry, as well as the imaginative openness claimed by Dickinson, leads to claims for its more fundamental artistry. It brings us back to a paradox that we will return to in Chapter 3: it is precisely the possession of fixed devices in poetry that enable it to achieve imaginative freedom by undermining them.

In considering the essential distinction between poetry and prose, we might see what the poets have said for poetry as against the exactitude of prose. One of the most engaging characterizations of poetry by an English writer comes in A. E. Housman's *The Name and Nature of Poetry*, mentioned already. Although Housman is not much associated with his modernist contemporaries, many

of his aesthetic judgements on poetry are strikingly like theirs.
He cites with approval Coleridge's observation that 'Poetry gives
most pleasure when only generally and not perfectly understood',
recalling Eliot's and Pound's recognition of 'the power of the
half-stated'. Housman goes on to say that 'meaning is of the
intellect, poetry is not', adding that 'poetry indeed seems to me
more physical than intellectual'. He cannot help us in the end in the
quest for a definition of poetry, saying that he 'could no more define
poetry than a terrier can define a rat': that is, it is something that
is done by instinct rather than calculation. This is a widely made
observation about poetry; the German Idealist philosopher
Friedrich Schelling said in the period of High Romanticism,
'Poetry is a union of the consciousness and the unconsciousness.'
But the real significance of Housman's poetics lies in the force
with which he emphasizes the physiological nature of poetry as a
motivation—the skin bristling while shaving—and his
corroboration of Wordsworth's opposing of poetry to the scientific:
'Poetry is not the thing said but a way of saying it'. It is another
version of the case for 'pure poetry'.

Housman's view of pure poetry has not escaped challenge
though, particularly what he says about a famous line from
Milton's *Arcades*:

> But in these six simple words of Milton—
>
> Nymphs and shepherds, dance no more—
>
> what is it that can draw tears, as I know it can, to the eyes of more
> readers than one?

F. W. Bateson, in his anti-Romantic *English Poetry: A Critical
Introduction*, says 'The pathos of Milton's six simple words
obviously derives for Housman from the last two of them', as
Shenstone had pointed out in the 18th century: 'the words "no
more" have a singular pathos; reminding us at once of past
pleasure, and the future exclusion of it'. Housman had also said

in his lecture, 'Take O take those lips away' is 'nonsense; but it is ravishing poetry'. Bateson is a great champion of sense and meaning in poetry, as pertaining to the intellect, and he (like the American poet-critic Yvor Winters) is an important counterblast to the view that poetry is of its nature irrational or anti-intellectual.

However, the Housman view that poetry is not of the intellect belongs in a long English tradition, even before the Romantic movement which Bateson blames for it. Edmund Burke said: 'it is the nature of all genius to be inexact'—something which has been repeatedly said of poetry in the 20th century. Even the practical Mill offers an inexact but suggestive aphorism: 'eloquence is heard, poetry is overheard'. He illustrates this with a musical parallel: Rossini is eloquence; Mozart and Beethoven are poetry. 'Who can imagine "Dove sono" *heard*? We imagine it overheard.' Similarly, Bateson unforgivingly quotes the hero of Aldous Huxley's *Those Barren Leaves* (1925), wondering 'What is it that makes the two words "defunctive music" as moving as the Dead March out of the *Eroïca* and the close of *Coriolan*...And the line, "Thoughts that do often lie too deep for tears"—why should its effect lie where it does? Mystery.'

All these subjective, epigrammatic observations are an evasion of definition, but also a claim for the specific, anti-prosaic nature of poetry. Among the poets there is general agreement that the poem cannot be forced into existence: Burns said, 'I have two or three times in my life composed from the wish rather than the impulse, but I never succeeded to any purpose'. Like Arnold's Scholar Gypsy, the poet waits 'for the spark from Heaven to fall', rather than following the 'wish' or intellect.

Many poets' observations reflect the uncertainties and inconclusiveness we have been finding here. Elizabeth Bishop says 'Writing poetry is an unnatural act', and that the challenge is to make it look natural. Marianne Moore said poetry consists of 'imaginary gardens with real toads in them'. In his wilful *ABC of Reading*, Ezra Pound (whose *Imagist Manifesto* particularly irritated Bateson) said poetry is 'News that stays news'. Poetry may be unprosaic or unscientific or unhistorical; but it does have its own realm of being, however elusive its contours are. The prose–poetry distinction raises the question of the prose poem which requires generic clarification. What is the effect of claiming the status of poetry for something which seems to be structured according to the rules of its syntactic antitype, in prose? Despite successful modern practitioners like Geoffrey Hill, the form of prose poem has not had the same prominence in English as in some other languages, notably French to which it seems native. The prose–poetry opposition seems more absolute in English.

Having attempted to distinguish it from prose or science or history, we might go on to ask where poetry has been found to have its distinctive application and its field of greatest authority. What are poets good at? And what are their obligations? It has been said to be a problem for theoreticians of language that they are attempting to be specialists in a field of which everyone is a practitioner. Something similar is true of the poet, as Valéry said: 'the poet's problem must be to derive from this instrument the means of creating a work essentially not practical' (the quality that is caught so well in Dickinson's poem opposing it to prose in general). In describing the technical difficulties for the poet, Valéry also contrasted the enviable condition of the composer of music, who can distinguish predictable, regular sounds from noise. The poet lacks the certitudes that the construction of music offers—scales, metronome, diapasons. 'He has nothing but the coarse instrument of the dictionary and the grammar.' So what can the poet achieve with these ambiguous instruments?

In using the words that everyone uses for communication and the expression of emotion, poetry can achieve an explicitness that music in itself or other formal arts, despite their regularity, cannot

50

match (unless of course we think of music, as some musicologists have, as being in origin linked with verbal expression, from which 'pure' music—what Anthony Storr calls 'Songs Without Words'—was the later derivative).

A famous consideration of the distinctive nature of poetry as an art, by contrast with the plastic arts—painting, sculpture, and architecture—was G. E. Lessing's 1766 'Essay on the Limits of Painting and Poetry', referred to by Matthew Arnold as 'Lessing's famed Laocoon'. In considering the killing of Laocoon and his sons by snakes as represented in sculpture and by Virgil in poetry, Lessing evaluates the relative strengths of the two arts: the verbal arts as allowing development through time by proceeding sequentially through sentences and lines, and the plastic arts by representing the whole of an event in a particular moment. Though he describes the strength of each, Lessing weights the argument in favour of poetry, with its capacity to develop and change.

This is an idea that reappears periodically through the history of aesthetics. In the early 20th century, Ezra Pound made much of the essay by Ernest Fenollosa on 'The Chinese Written Character as a Medium for Poetry'. Although Fenollosa's analysis is often questioned by other commentators, the English poet Donald Davie in his influential 1975 book on the syntax of poetry, *Articulate Energy*, says that 'Fenollosa's little treatise is perhaps the only English document of our time fit to rank with Sidney's *Apologie*, and the Preface to the *Lyrical Ballads*, and Shelley's *Defence*, the great poetic manifestos of the past'. Fenollosa says that 'one superiority of verbal poetry as an *art* rests in its getting back to the fundamental reality of *time*'. In literature movement through time is most usually associated with longer narrative structures and developments of plot. But of course shorter poems too proceed word by word through a kinetic sequence. The later 20th century saw a developing interest in ekphrastic poetry, poems that described in their development forms that paintings

2. Arundel Tomb at Chichester Cathedral.

and sculptures represent as a fixed, unmoving tableau. Famous examples are Auden's 'Musée des Beaux Arts', responding to Bruegel's painting 'Landscape with the Fall of Icarus', and Rainer Maria Rilke's 'Archaic Torso of Apollo'.

Philip Larkin's 'An Arundel Tomb', one of the most popular modern English poems, is a classic of the ekphrastic form, illustrating Lessing's opposition perfectly. The poem describes the figures on a tomb in Chichester Cathedral (see Figure 2); the tomb is dated to Chaucer's time, the late 14th century, though it was significantly restored in the mid-19th century. (Larkin later expressed gloomy dissatisfaction with the poem for getting the artistic history of the monument wrong.) The poem starts with a statement of what the viewer sees in the cathedral:

> Side by side, their faces blurred,
> The Earl and Countess lie in stone.

This conventional representation of knight in armour and his lady is described as the 'plainness of the pre-Baroque' which 'hardly involves the eye' until

> One sees, with a sharp tender shock,
>> His hand withdrawn, holding her hand.

The movement from what is seen at first glance, to the shock of this later view of the personal contact can only be described in words; the material image itself can't change.

Fenollosa claims that Chinese poetry with its ideograms builds into pictorial representation of the physical objects the notion of movement from one moment to another. Pound, in his development of imagism as a poetic form, follows him in making the claim that English poetry (in a language which is similarly low in grammatical inflexions) can operate in the same way. The most celebrated imagist poem is Pound's 1913 'In a Station of the Metro':

> The apparition of these faces in the crowd;
>> Petals on a wet, black bough.

The collocation of these two lines, as in other imagist poems, serves to frustrate the reader's natural inclination to link the ideas together logically. (It is interesting that one early version of the poem has a colon rather than a semi-colon at the end of the first line, which might be construed as an indication of simultaneity rather than the change of state or sequentiality suggested by the semi-colon. Are the petals an image for the faces, or the next thing observed in time? Are the lines sequential, or are they in apposition?) Pound's two-line poem, especially with the colon of the original version, wants the lines to behave more like painting in Lessing's terms by putting two pictures side by side without any active movement between them. But language of its nature can't hold back from making connections as one set of words follows another.

The issues raised here have been addressed in various terms through artistic history; the Roman poet Horace said *ut pictura poesis*—a poem must attempt to attain the stability and fixity of a picture. But the English writer Walter Pater in the late 19th century said, 'All art constantly aspires towards the condition of music', which, given music's essential movement through time, recalls Lessing's distinction again and seems to question it.

In all these cases what we are asking is what context we might expect to find poetry dominant in—if it is not the realm of the scientific where prose is the normal language. Mr Keating in the film *Dead Poets' Society* says poetry was invented to woo women; it has certainly had a long, apparently universal relationship with love, if not necessarily (or even usually) to woo women. Love in its various senses has been a major preoccupation for all the arts including literature, and not least for poetry.

As for love poetry, it is worth remarking that once again we find the discussion and practice of Chinese poetry echoing, or anticipating, the Western tradition to a striking degree. For example we cannot fail to be reminded of the celebrated eccentricities of Western love poetry when we read that, despite the emphasis in accounts of Chinese poetry on the poems that deal with the profession of affection between men, according to James Liu 'many men did feel true love for women, if not always for their wives, and there *is* a great deal of love poetry in Chinese'. Here yet again is the 'Courtly Love' that used to be said to be an invention of 11th-century Provence, just as we find it cropping up again throughout the following millennium in Europe and the Middle East. This is not love poetry as defined by Mr Keating, but it does share the abstraction and impracticality of the European courtly tradition. Love clearly is one of the contexts where we must expect to find poetry.

But what kinds of love? Shelley, in one of his most beautiful and delicate lyrics, takes on in verse what he pronounced on in prose in the *Defence of Poetry*:

> I can give not what men call love;
> But wilt thou accept not
> The worship the heart lifts above
> And the Heavens reject not:
> The desire of the moth for the star,
> Of the night for the morrow,
> The devotion to something afar
> From the sphere of our sorrow?

Here the distinction between 'what men call love' and the grand, transcendent 'worship' that the poet can offer is strikingly reminiscent of the discussion of love in general, from Plato to the Romantics. Love seems to be an invariable home ground for poetry—particularly love of an exalted and numinous kind. The last line of Dante's *Commedia* identifies God as the love that moves the sun and the other stars, making the frequent and complex association between religious love and bodily love, an association which is not always easy to disentangle, perhaps as part of the legacy of poetry as ritual: with some of the love poets of the high Middle Ages, from the Troubadours to Dante, it is often difficult to be certain which is the field of application.

Another of poetry's apparently universal areas of speciality, to rival that of love, is nature. Somewhere between devotion to truth and to pleasure comes the question of fidelity to nature, as in the *OED*'s definition 1 of poetry—'Adherence to the truth of nature'—which was also central to Sidney's discussion when he says: 'There is no art delivered to mankind that hath not the works of Nature for his principal object, without which they could not consist.' The 19th-century American transcendentalist Ralph Waldo Emerson said that poetry is a kind of equivalent to nature, a pre-existing entity that it is for the poet to create out of. And one of the best known literary aphorisms in English is Pope's definition of 'True wit', again from his 'Essay on Criticism':

> True wit is Nature to advantage drest:
> What oft was thought but ne'er so well expressed.

Nature of course is itself a complex and uncertain term, and we will consider in Chapter 4 fidelity to nature as one of the functions of poetry which competes with moral seriousness in importance. Shelley's love, the 'word too often profaned' in the first line of the poem I have just quoted, is universal in nature: the natural and instinctive 'desire of the moth for the star' as well as the human 'devotion to something afar | From the sphere of our sorrow'.

So *is* nature, in some sense, the essential and primal subject of art, including poetry? And what exactly does nature mean in this context? What do we expect from 'nature poetry'? We have already noted Emerson's view that poetry is a kind of equivalent to nature, a pre-existing entity that the poet can create from. Somewhere between devotion to truth and to pleasure comes the question of fidelity to nature, as in the *OED*'s definition, and also central to Sidney's discussion. In Aristotle's claims for poetry as an imitation of nature he is referring to the whole of the perceived and sensible world. Again, though Chinese, Japanese, and Korean poetry resemble European traditions of nature poetry in ways that have been found resonant for the West, nature is explored there in much more intently detailed ways, without the wider metaphysical implications of Aristotle or Sidney.

But does nature, in the sense in which it is fundamental to poetry, mean things of the natural world, as distinct from things of the mind and reason: the things we found listed by Confucius, quoted in the Introduction: 'birds, beasts, herbs, and trees'? Sidney goes on to say that the following of nature is not the highest thing that poetry does. The great achievement of the poet is that he,

> disdaining to be tied to any such subjection [to nature, as other arts
> are], lifted up with the vigour of his own invention, doth grow in
> effect another nature, in making things either better than Nature
> bringeth forth, or, quite anew, forms such as never were in Nature,
> as the heroes, demi-gods, Cyclops, Chimeras, Furies, and such like.
> Nature's world is brazen, the poets only deliver a golden.

Here once again, even if it is in different terms, we have the second grand claim for poetry, side by side with Shelley's unacknowledged legislators: what Coleridge in his 'Dejection' ode memorably called the 'shaping spirit of Imagination'. Although that phrase has been mainly associated with the Romantics, it is an aphoristic formulation for the 'making' capacity that has always been claimed for the artists in the Western tradition. Wordsworth and Coleridge agreed about 'the two cardinal points of poetry, the power of exciting the sympathy of the reader by a faithful adherence to the truth of nature, and the power of giving the interest of novelty by the modifying colours of imagination'. Roger Kuin celebrates Sidney's *Apologie* 'for its faculty of "invention" which makes poesy, alone among human arts and sciences, the equal of creating Nature, under God'. Hence the recurrence of such 'making' words for the poet as the Greek *poietes*, the Anglo-Saxon *scop*, and the medieval-Renaissance English and Scots term 'makar, maker'. In claiming such a capacity for poets, they are being seen as beyond nature: supernatural.

Chapter 3
The language of poetry and its particular devices

There are clearly certain 'arrangements of language' (to use the terms of the *OED* definition) that are particularly associated with poetry—effects of sound and figuration for example: such things as rhyme or alliteration or metaphor. Whether poetry is thought to be imitative-realistic or transcendent, all discussions agree that it must have *some* kinds of rules and recognized practices: the things that contribute to what Mill called 'something peculiar in its nature'. Otherwise we could not define it at all as what it is, or know what to do to create it in practice. The rules link to the debates about language and which areas of language they may—or may not—apply to: rules about the sounds of poetry—metre or scansion or rhyme; or about its linguistic structure—its grammar or word-formation. These are things that occur in language in general, but are often thought to have special application in poetry where special rules of usage are likelier than usual to occur.

But a much more contentious question is whether there is some kind of *reserved* language, peculiar to poetry: the kind of language that belongs to literature in particular that Derek Attridge identifies in his book *Peculiar Language*. Terry Eagleton says 'If you approach me at a bus-stop and murmur "Thou still unravished bride of quietness", then I am instantly aware that I am in the presence of the literary.' His example of the literary here is a famous piece of poetry (by Keats), and the qualities he goes on to list rather vaguely ('the texture, rhythm and resonance of your words') apply particularly to poetry, so it seems that within the literary it is poetry, if anything, that has a special language.

Is there then generally a language that is encountered in poetry which is not found in everyday usage at all? Once again the argument between Wordsworth and Coleridge is at the heart of the matter: between Wordsworth's claim that poetry should use the language of 'a man speaking to men', as against Coleridge's declaration that the language of poetry cannot be the language of normal speech: 'There may be, is, and ought to be, an essential difference between the language of prose and of metrical composition.'

If so, what are its rules? Attempts to resolve this argument have sometimes fallen back on linguistic properties: for example the linguist Roman Jakobson said that a distinctive feature of poetry is that in it 'the devices are the heroes'; the linguistic special effects—the departures from the norms of usage—are the crucial factor in marking poetic language off from normal language. Generally, in language as well as everything else (in grammar and spelling, for instance), observance of rules is a positive thing, but poetry often achieves its effects by breaching the rules. The French American critic Michael Riffaterre described all these effects as 'ungrammaticalities'. Indeed, it was said that the formulation of grammatical and idiomatic rules in neoclassical periods such as the 18th century had the ironic advantage for poets like Keats that they were able to achieve stylistic effects by breaking them. Keats's reviewers may have objected to his grammatical solecisms—verbless sentences in *Endymion*, or his idiomatic breaches of decorum or propriety, like 'empty some dull opiate to the *drains*'; but such things were one of the staples of his poetic style.

To take a much-cited modern example, in Dylan Thomas's poem 'A Grief Ago', the title- phrase is very effective though it is strictly speaking idiomatically wrong. Between 'a' and 'ago' the language requires a time reference, such as 'hour' or 'day' or 'year' or 'while'. The breach of the rule here turns 'grief' into a matter of time: which of course, when we think about it, it is in one sense. But it took the poet's aberrant usage to make us think about it and we recognize this as something poetry does particularly effectively, making us intensely aware of something we already know by presenting it in an unfamiliar way. To express this, the rather cumbersome term 'defamiliarization' has been developed: cumbersome, but precisely accurate, meaning to achieve something out of the ordinary in what appears to be ordinary.

What Thomas does here is a breach in idiom; elsewhere he employs what we might think of as similarly defamiliarizing poetic effects by departing from the norms of grammar or syntax. An example is his best known line, the opening of his great elegy for his father, 'Do not go gentle into that good night'. Strictly we might expect the adverbial form 'gently' rather than the adjectival 'gentle'. And there is a subtle breach of idiom and meaning too: we take the closing three words to refer to death; yet the phrase 'good night' is normally an end-of-day farewell (wonderfully expressive in this context of course), and it can't normally have the demonstrative adjective 'that' to qualify it.

Both of these examples from Thomas suggest that the breach of rule in poetic usage must not simply break the rule for the sake of it: the unfamiliar usage must introduce a new effectiveness, such as the aptness of a time reference applied to grief, or of valediction in the phrase 'good night'. Moreover, there are some rules that can never be broken for poetic effect; we can't, for instance, change the word order of 'dog bites man' to 'man bites dog' and retain its sense (as we could in Latin: *canis virum mordet* means the same as *virum canis mordet*).

Some rules in language are said to be 'in free variation': that is, we can change them round without affecting the meaning we are aiming at. Spellings such as 'connexion' and 'connection' are examples. Neither could be said to be wrong. But again, poetry has an uncertain relationship with these variants. e. e. cummings uses capital or lower-case letters in a way that is not normal in spelling (or 'orthography', to use the term that means correct or orthodox writing); it is not clear what Emily Dickinson means by using dashes as she does. John Fuller raises the question of capitalization at the start of lines of poetry (which he favours): is this a purely typographical matter, or is there some semantic significance?

The whole matter of correctness in written forms is a complex one, once we have conceded that poets are at liberty to break the normal rules of language. An interesting case is the spelling of Yeats's poems. Yeats enthusiasts are very insistent that his eccentric spelling should not be seen as evidence of dyslexia; both in his own time and since, his aberrant spellings have usually been silently corrected (though they are increasingly left as Yeats wrote them, especially in the magisterial volumes of his letters edited by John Kelly). But are they to be seen as calculated variants, and departures from the norm? The dilemma is clearer with grammatical, rather than orthographic, aberrations where editors have to decide. One of Yeats's most admired and influential poems, 'The Second Coming', ends

but now I know
That twenty centuries of stony sleep
Were vexed to nightmare by a rocking cradle,
And what rough beast, its hour come round at last,
Slouches towards Bethlehem to be born?

This seems to be a statement ('now I know...what rough beast...Slouches towards Bethlehem'), but the sentence ends with a question-mark, prompted (strictly wrongly) by the apparently interrogative 'what' in the penultimate line. No modern editor would change the punctuation here—as Warburton did of

Shakespeare, or Bentley of Milton, in the prescriptive 18th century. In *King Lear*, Warburton—and other editors—changed the phrase 'in the restoring his bereaved sense' because 'the' has to be followed by a noun which therefore must be what 'restoring' is; but 'restoring' is also a transitive verb because it governs the direct object 'sense'. Is it a noun or a verb? Hence our grammatical rule: either 'playing games' (present participle of the verb with its direct object); or 'the playing of games', the verbal noun. But of course nobody would now debar poetry from making such 'mistakes' in using what were called such 'mixed constructions'. Breach of rule is now seen as an essential part of the poet's equipment.

To widen the question of whether poetry has a language particular to it we might ask whether there are rules of operation for poetry at all, or whether it can be left to a spontaneous outpouring. Are there general rules—rules which must be invariably observed—in any poetic traditions? Here, yet again, we find that Aristotle has anticipated later discussions with authority and cogency. His priority here was shown convincingly by Umberto Eco, who takes back to Aristotle the series of paradoxes and contradictions that beset the discussion of poetic rule. In his essay 'The *Poetics* and Us', Eco sees the essence of the problem in the claim that poetry is required to be rule-governed but also somehow spontaneous (leading to the claim for transcendence: its emergence seems to come from outside us). The most important challenge for the poet, according to Aristotle, is to strike a balance between poetry's claims for truth and its formal observation of the rules of the art.

Eco's central text for debate here is the extraordinary essay *The Philosophy of Composition* by Edgar Allan Poe, in which Poe 'explains the rule whereby he managed to convey the impression of spontaneity'. In this essay Poe rationalizes the gestation of his famous poem 'The Raven' in a very dubious manner, by showing its surreal form to be the logical product of a series of practical aesthetic decisions. Writing poetry, it seems, is a matter of learning the rules according to which the writer can fake unruledness. This notion of course, as Eco says, has a long history in the discussion of rhetoric: rhetoric is the more assertive discourse that Mill calls eloquence when he says that 'Eloquence is heard; poetry is overheard'. Indeed, the creative evasion of the normal rules of language and rhetoric has often been seen as one of the most influential views of poetics in the 20th century, especially as developed by Jakobson.

The style and register of English poetry

Even if it is accepted that there is a distinctive language reserved for poetry in general, we might go on to ask: is there a particular kind of language that characterizes English poetry? C. S. Lewis said brilliantly of a rather obscure line of Chaucer that it contains in seed the whole style of subsequent English poetry:

Singest with vois memorial in the shade.

The achievement of style here is indeed very characteristic of the effects of register (in the sense of stylistic level) prized in English, perhaps largely attributable to its hybrid Germanic-Italic origins: the way the Old English words 'sing' and 'shade' are wrapped round the French borrowings 'vois' and 'memorial' captures the essential mix that the modern English lexicon is composed of.

Such stylistic variation in the use of source language has been highly productive in the history of English, in prose as well as verse. There is a wonderfully rich example early in Sir Thomas Browne's *Hydriotaphia, or Urn-Buriall* (the variant etymological names of which of course are themselves an instance of this rich polyphony): pondering on Roman urns that have been dug up near Norwich, Browne—a writer who has an indisputable claim to a place among Sidney's 'most excellent poets that never versified'—reflects that 'Time, which antiquates antiquities and hath an art to make dust of all things, hath yet spared these minor monuments'. As in Chaucer's line, the two Latin-derived phrases 'antiquates antiquities' and 'minor monuments' are wrapped round the run of fourteen monosyllables, all but one of which ('art') are derived from Old English. In the Chaucer line, it is not only the etymology that achieves poetic effect: the French-derived 'vois memorial' is an inversion of the English adjective–noun word order. And the play of monosyllables and polysyllables (as in Browne where it is reinforced by alliteration) has its own music, whatever source language it comes from.

We might recall again the insistence by writers from Aristotle to Sidney to Mill that some prose can be more poetic than verse that rhymes and features other formalities. Such counterpoint is at the heart of Shakespeare's lexical style: maybe the most frequently cited example is Macbeth's

> this my hand will rather
> The multitudinous seas incarnadine,
> Making the green one red,

where again the two Latinate polysyllabic terms are made more effective by contrast with the Anglo-Saxon monosyllables in the lines preceding and following.

If these instances tempt us to revisit the Wordsworth–Coleridge distinction between the language of poetry (and other literary registers) and normal speech, we should remember that from its medieval origins English has exploited constructively the possibility of stylistic felicity in playing off such components of word-formation against each other. In general, from the 16th century to Matthew Arnold at the end of the 19th, there has been a preference for 'plain Anglo-Saxon' over what Arnold called the 'lubricity', the slipperiness, of French: a prejudice which was openly declared even by writers who demonstrably did not act on it in their own practice. The preference for the plain Anglo-Saxon extended to a claim for truth (which recalls Plato's strictures on poetry), famously celebrated in Foxe's *Book of Martyrs*.

The words given by Foxe to Hugh Latimer, burnt at Oxford in 1555, to address his fellow martyr Nicholas Ridley, are a classic and much-quoted instance: 'Play the man, Master Ridley; we shall this day light such a candle, by God's grace, in England, as I trust shall never be put out.'

This unadorned prose language has found favour with commentators on English poetry too, sometimes by contrast even with Milton whose ringing magnificence in *Paradise Lost* has often been accused of foreignness in English. Samuel Johnson says of Milton in *The Lives of the Poets* that 'both in prose and verse, he had formed his style by a perverse and pedantic principle', but 'such is the power of his poetry that his call is obeyed without resistance, the reader feels himself in captivity to a higher and nobler mind, and criticism sinks in admiration'. Johnson continues with this ambivalence towards Milton's 'grace in its deformity', quoting Samuel Butler's calling his language 'a Babylonish dialect', but concludes that Milton 'has selected the melodious words with such diligence that from his book alone [*Paradise Lost*] the Art of English Poetry might be learned' (as Lewis said it might be from Chaucer).

In the discussion of English poetry it is almost inevitable to encounter Milton in connexion with enhanced or specialist diction. Early in the 20th century, T. S. Eliot and F. R. Leavis raised something of a sacrilegious critical storm by criticizing Milton's language for what Eliot called 'the hypertrophy of the auditory imagination'; that is, for using a language that was more sonorous than pictorial—the language that Tennyson had admired when he called Milton the 'mighty-mouthed inventor of harmonies'.

Clearly, one of the great strengths of English as a language for poetry—or for any artistic expression—is its double lexical structure. It equipped Milton to write 'in hideous ruin and combustion down | to bottomless perdition' in *Paradise Lost*, as well as the great plainstyle last line of the sonnet 'On His

Blindness'—'They also serve who only stand and wait.' In exploiting this lexical double structure, Milton was—as we have seen—preceded by Chaucer whose style at the outset of post-Conquest English poetry is already a miracle of various expressiveness.

Lascelles Abercrombie, in his admirable (and now largely forgotten) 1925 book, *The Idea of Great Poetry*, demonstrated the same gift as Lewis's for spotting a memorable and effective line (a skill characteristic of critics of the 1920s and 1930s generation) in choosing for praise the line describing the clearance made by the cutting down of the trees in Chaucer's *Knight's Tale*:

> Ne how the ground agast was of the light.

Here the operative word is 'agast', the origin of the modern 'aghast', derived from Old English. The extraordinary *meaning* of the line is that the ground, normally protected from the light by the trees, is shocked by the glare when the trees are cut down (an idea which is particularly resonant in our time when there is such anxiety about the destruction of the rainforests and so much pictorial representation of it): the *OED* says 'aghast' means 'filled with sudden fright or horror'. It is a wonderful piece of anthropomorphism, something of which Chaucer is a great master, when human sentiments are applied to the extra-human world: here not just to any part of the world, but to the animate world. Chaucer has been found a rich resource for the seekers out of great lines. The wholly Anglo-Saxon vocabulary of the line describing the assassin in the Temple of Mars in *The Knight's Tale*—'The smiler with the knife under the cloke'—was singled out for admiration by several writers in that *mot juste* period early in the 20th century, including Housman who contrasted it with the verbose 'refining' of it in Dryden's translation:

> Next stood Hypocrisy, with holy leer,
> Soft smiling and demurely looking down,
> But hid the dagger underneath the gown.

However, to support the view that poetry needs some special verbal effects to achieve its ends and can't simply rely on its Anglo-Saxon plainness, we might recall a celebrated piece of spoof verse by Johnson who offered this quatrain as something that looks like poetry and meets the metrical requirements, but certainly doesn't qualify as poetry in any exalted sense: not the product of a candidate for political legislating.

> I put my hat upon my head
> And walked into the Strand.
> And there I met another man
> Whose hat was in his hand.

What exactly disqualifies this pleasant jingle from consideration as poetry? We don't want to be forced into requiring solemnity of matter or the like; and of course this encounter in the Strand *could* be developed into something of significance. For example, the other man might have taken his hat off in a venerating response to a celestial vision. Neither do we want to make the oddness or specialness of vocabulary an essential; the last line of Milton's Sonnet 'On His Blindness' just quoted—'They also serve who only stand and wait'—attains its great power without using anything out of the ordinary verbally; it attains its effect by a simplicity that departs from the more contorted grammar and register established in the earlier parts of the poem: 'who best bear his mild yoke, they serve him best', for example.

It should be said too that, while English has gained its contrapuntal expressiveness and variety from its hybrid origins, there is another kind of variety that its dependence on word order for meaning means it can't naturally attain. One of the commonest solecisms in imperfectly written English poetry is inversion (the 'my heart to her gave I' sort of thing), which often can't be used in English without loss of logical sense as well as idiomatic naturalness. There is of course some validation in major poets for emphatic inversion for stylistic effect where the meaning is unaffected. Tennyson's line, quoted for its sonority later on here—'Dry clash'd his harness in the icy caves'—and Milton's 'Him the almighty power | Hurled headlong flaming from the ethereal sky', both reverse the obligatory subject–verb–object order in a way that would not be acceptable in normal speech. We might suggest that some syntactic usages are in 'free variation' (like the spellings of 'judgement/judgment' or 'connexion/connection', mentioned already) in poetry in a way that they are not normally, operating in the same way as other breaches of rule function in poetry.

But inversion is at the heart of the impact of Latin style—in Ciceronian prose as well as in verse. To take a very popular pair of lines by Catullus,

> Nobis cum semel occidit brevis lux
> nox est perpetua una dormienda.

This is an extreme example of the 'syntactical reordering' that the *OED* identified; a word-for-word English translation would be something like 'For us, when at last dies the brief light, a night is perpetual, single to be slept', which clearly will not do in English. There are simpler examples in Latin and French: Lucretius's title *De rerum natura* would translate as *Concerning of Things the Nature*. We might even say that the stylistic clarity that English attains through its semantic word order comes at a stylistic price. This is certainly suggested by the frequency with which aspiring poets choose inversions that are not natural to English. In particular I think the impossibility of emulating the syntactic sinuosity of the Latin-derived languages loses something highly expressive in poetry which English does not easily replace. The writing of John Donne offers successful attempts to achieve such styles in English:

> As well a well-wrought urn becomes
> The greatest ashes as half-acre tombs.

'As well' has been brought up to the start, rather than in its logical place after 'ashes'. Similarly,

> Richly cloth'd Apes are called Apes, and as soon
> Eclips'd as bright we call the Moon the Moon.

'We call the Moon the Moon' (already an improbable, if brilliant, repetition) should come before 'as soon'. If the history of English has given it certain lexical and phonetic strengths (counterpoint and a monosyllabic clarity), other languages have different stylistic strengths which English strains to emulate.

As a last structural feature typical of English, it is often said that the language is deficient in rhymes. In fact this isn't quite true: English is rich in monosyllabic rhymes, but it is not willing to rhyme the polysyllables that are produced by Latin-derived inflexions. Therefore English finds Dante hard to translate rhyme for rhyme because of Italian's acceptance of inflexional rhyming. As Osip Mandelstam says of Dante, 'The abundance of marriageable endings is fantastic'. In *Inferno* 1 for instance, the inflexional ending of '*durata*' (lasted) is rhymed with '*affannata*' (panted) in a way which English has never naturalized—except in popular folk-songs, such as the Irish 'The Boys of Mullabaun':

> Without a hesitation
> We are charged with combination
> And sent for transportation
> From the hills of Mullabaun.

All languages have their own structures that equip them to achieve particular effects of style. Since the inflexional system in Latin indicates the grammatical status of every word—as subject or object, or as present or past tense—it is possible for Latin writers to achieve variety and fluency by swapping around word order. Since it lost much of its inflexional system in the Middle Ages, English has to attain variety and inventiveness by other means. Something which is perhaps linked to the matter of lexical distribution and which has attracted a good deal of attention in the recent criticism of poetry is verbal repetition, which English seems more forgiving of than it is of Latinate inversion or polysyllabic rhyming. Of course repetition in general is of the greatest importance in the rhythmic structure of poetry; *The Princeton Handbook of Poetic Terms* calls it 'the basic unifying device in all poetry'. The Donne example just quoted collocates 'the Moon the Moon' in a way that is unlikely to occur in normal usage. Seamus Heaney (a writer whose syntax is often influenced by Donne's which he greatly admired) has a striking repetition of the kind: a book in Braille is said to be 'Like books the books of wallpaper-patterns came in.'

Such improbably distributed verbal repetition ('books the books') is not the same kind of thing as the rhythmic repetitions the *Princeton Handbook* is referring to (things like refrains or thematic recurrences or rhyme); it is more like the devices that depart from the norms of usage we were looking at earlier in Dylan Thomas or Keats. But why are these statistically improbable recurrences or repetitions of words found satisfying in English poetry? Perhaps it is related to the centrality of ritual in the whole discussion. Clearly a satisfactory explanation would require a fuller consideration of the word-formation and word order of different languages.

Imagery, tropes, and schemes

In Chapter 1, we noted that both Frost and Aristotle say that the tendency to image making and the metaphorical was the essence of the poetic. As well as the examples of the lexical effects of register, in which, as we have seen, English is exceptionally rich because of its double structure with its Germanic origins overlaid and enriched by Latinate vocabulary, English uses its multiplicity of sources to develop a distinctive poetic imagery. This is not a simple term and it is not easy to define. What exactly is an image (rather like earlier terms such as 'conceit' as applied to the usage by Donne and the metaphysicals of far-fetched comparisons, or the 'blason' derived from heraldry)?

This uncertainty is evident in the very different subjects of such books as C. Day-Lewis's *The Poetic Image* and Frank Kermode's *Romantic Image*. They hardly seem to be talking about the same thing. Kermode is concerned with the kind of figurative effects inherited by Yeats from the French *symbolistes* while Day-Lewis is examining the metaphorical effects that are 'at the core of the poem'. Day-Lewis's understanding of 'image' is roughly equivalent to the metaphysical conceit, or the kind of extended metaphor that has been said to be the central idea in a particular Shakespeare play (like clothes as fitness for office in *Macbeth*), while Kermode uses the term to refer to the kind of symbolic idea that a word is forced to carry in a particular context (like the chestnut tree at the end of Yeats's 'Among School Children').

We might return to Abercrombie for another of his choice passages, Fletcher's beautiful description of a scatter of rose-leaves on the stream:

> And on the water, like to burning coals
> On liquid silver, leaves of roses lay.

The appeal of this is not a matter of vocabulary but of perception: the appearance of the red rose-leaves is evoked by the richly imaginative simile of burning coals on molten silver, all the more effective for being invented (burning coals are never literally seen in the setting of silver). In imagery it seems the appeal is to the eye—what Hamlet calls 'the mind's eye'—as the sound devices of poetry (rhyme, alliteration, and so on) are to the ear.

If the answer to the question of the effectiveness of similitude in poetry lies in what Wallace Stevens says in 'The Man with the Blue Guitar', that

> Things as they are
> are changed upon my blue guitar,

this does not explain *why* we want this change to happen (even if it is one of the most satisfying expressions of defamiliarization in a poem in English). Seamus Heaney was praised from the first for his capacity to describe in language things as they are: the vivid description of holly that 'gleamed like smashed bottle-glass', for example. But, immediate as the impact is there, it is still effected by the operation of a simile. In a very interesting discussion of the figurative in her book *The Art of Poetry: How to Read a Poem* (2001), Shira Wolosky uses the term 'Incomplete Figures' to suggest that what the use of figures and symbols does is not to describe things as what they are not, but to use a term that describes them incompletely under one, but not all, of their aspects. Holly is like bottle-glass in its colour and perhaps in its sharpness, but unlike it in all other respects. Wolosky's term accounts suggestively for the way that a figure only partly delineates its referent.

More traditionally, it has been claimed that precisely what poetry does is to give us a sharper sense of reality, of 'things as they are', by changing the terms in which they are described. This was most famously said by the Russian formalist critic Victor Shklovsky, whose term for what poetry does is usually translated into English as the 'defamiliarization' mentioned earlier. At its best, our perception of the world is vivid and sensual, but a literal representation finds it hard to recreate that perception: in Shklovsky's famous expression of it, 'to make the stone *stony*'. This is what art attempts to do: to convert something from the physical world into language. How does this idea work as a description of what is happening in the passage from Fletcher?

Some commentators on figuration and symbolism distinguish between alteration of diction in single words (tropes) and in longer units of syntax and grammar (sometimes called schemes).

The idea of schemes describes another way in which language in poetry seems to function differently from the way it normally does: in Chapter 4, in considering the genres of poetry, we will see there are ways in which the same effects can occur in the more extended genres, epic and drama—for example by Derek Walcott in *Omeros* and some lyric poems that draw on Homeric episodes.

In considering the question of correctness in language, Noam Chomsky devised a famous sentence to be scrutinized for its correctness or 'acceptability': 'Colourless green ideas sleep furiously'. The semantic contradictions ('colourless/green'; 'ideas/sleep'; 'sleep/furiously') prompt us to say that the sentence is incorrect or unacceptable. But it is correct grammatically: adjective–adjective–noun–verb–adverb, as in 'Tall young people run quickly'. More significantly, it is easy to suggest a poetic context in which it operates metaphorically. For example, the word 'colourless' in the metaphorical sense—something like 'without marked characteristics'—does not conflict in meaning with the word 'green' (which, for that matter, could mean 'unripe' or 'guileless'). So Chomsky's sentence, deliberately chosen for the contradictions it sets up in purely literal terms, is after all acceptable both grammatically and metaphorically. Challenges of this kind are commonly made in poetry workshops: think of a poetic context in which a contradictory proposition will work—'ice is very hot', for instance, could be salvaged metaphorically by the addition 'compared to your indifference to me'. There are stranger things in Wallace Stevens than Chomsky's sentence. So we might say that a poetic context—recognizing the 'poetic' as the literary identified by Eagleton at the start of this chapter—changes the linguistic function of the sentence. Decisions about the place of the literal and the figurative are at the linguistic heart of the definition of poetry.

If abstruse effects of imagery are, like register, more influential and favoured in some languages than others, it remains striking how the same devices occur across poetic traditions which seem to have little historical or geographical context in common. An understanding of its context—its era and culture and genre—is essential for the interpretation of any poetry; but some kinds of imagery seem to work in the same way in very different cultures. As an extreme example, we might consider the aesthetic echoes in figurative effects between some varieties of short Chinese poems and poems in the Western tradition: imagist poems like Pound's, for example, or poems by Emily Dickinson or William Carlos Williams. (Several 20th-century American poets, such as Gary Snyder and Charles Olson, build on this affinity.) The affinity is remarkable given that the quality I am talking about seems inherent in the linguistic structure of Chinese—its grammar—while it occurs against the grammatical grain of the English or American practitioners.

In illustrating the untranslatability of some Chinese poems into English, Raymond Dawson gives an element-for-element translation of a 5th-century poem by Wu Mai-yüan, describing the sentiments of a young wife separated from her husband:

> flowering lacks plant tree gladness
> affliction exhausts frost dew sadness

Dawson translates:

> My flowering prime is deprived even of the vegetable happiness
>   of trees and flowers;
> Yet in my bitterness I taste all the hardships of blighting frost.

For the reader of Western literature, what is most striking here is the fact that it shares with the European tradition precisely the response to the change of seasons that has prevailed from the Middle Ages to *The Waste Land*: that the lovelorn figure cannot share the organic happiness of the natural world. Eliot's April is the cruellest month mainly because there is no fulfilling human equivalent to the tubers that are produced by physical nature.

Chaucer's 'folk' long 'to gon on pilgrimages' as an analogical
response to the sexual excitement of the birds that 'slepen al the
niht with open eye'. A much loved Middle English lyric is a lament
of the same kind:

> Foweles in the frith;
> Fishes in the flod;
> And I must waxe wod.
> Much sorrow I dwell with
> For beste of bone and blood.

(In modern English: 'birds in the forest, fishes in the stream, and
I must go crazy. I live in great sorrow for the best creature made of
bone and blood.')

So the Chinese poem has its Western equivalents in both form and
meaning. It is, as Dawson says, a strikingly complex structure of
thought. But the unexpanded, word-for-word version is not so
foreign either to these medieval poems in theme, or in structure to
imagist poems by American imagists such as Carlos Williams or
Amy Lowell. In the Chinese poem as in Western imagist poems of
the kind, the assembling of the meaning seems to fall back on the
addition of a linking syntax to fill it out, a syntax which may or
may not underlie the poem's grammar. Lowell's 'Yoshirawa
Lament' has a similar disconnectedness:

> Golden peacocks
> Under blossoming cherry-trees,
> But on all the wide sea
> There is no boat.

The Chinese poem has affinities too with the poems of Emily
Dickinson:

> It tossed—and tossed—
> A little Brig I knew—o'ertook by Blast—

It spun—and spun—
And groped delirious, for Morn—
It slipped—and slipped—
As One that drunken—stept—
Its white foot tripped—
Then dropped from sight—
Ah, Brig—Good Night
To crew and You—
The Ocean's Heart too smooth—too Blue—
To break for You—

It is a different order of crypticism and incompleteness of course:
Dickinson's poetry is never wholly like anything else. But all these
poems require some kind of syntactic expansion in the course
of interpretation which establishes them as the same sort of
ontological form. They are all more like each other than they are
like *Paradise Lost* or Homer's *Odyssey* or even—more tellingly—a
Renaissance sonnet or a poem by Andrew Marvell with its
complex but logical syntactic organization. (I mention Marvell
because Dickinson's poems can seem influenced by the
development of thought of poems like 'The Definition of Love':
the verbal quality that T. S. Eliot memorably called 'a tough
reasonableness beneath the slight lyric grace'.)

There are a great number of books on what we might call the
special effects of poetry in English—on metre and rhyme and
alliteration. Any discussion of the language of poetry must of
course deal with versification and poetics. Even though all the
authorities from Aristotle to Mill to John Hollander agree that
it is an inadequate definition of poetry to equate it with 'metrical
composition', it is striking, and not inappropriate, that a very
high proportion of the handbooks of poetry concern themselves
precisely with that. This is not just because the devices of such
composition are more identifiable and tractable (it is much
easier to define alliteration or rhyme than 'the poetic'); it is
undeniable that form is of great importance within all particular

Poetry

76

poems and for the writer's sense of what they are doing in composing poems.

It is important too to remember that the formalities of poetry—the special devices it uses—are not only a matter of rhyme and metre and phonetic effects—the things sometimes referred to collectively as 'prosody'. There are other fundamental things—to which of course these prosodic effects may contribute: such things as repetition and statement of the obvious—that occur to a greater extent than in normal usage. There are various kinds of patterning, both in the forms of words and in their combination.

Perhaps the most important issue here is similitude, as claimed by Aristotle: the degree to which things are compared to other things in art—what Wallace Stevens in *The Necessary Angel* calls analogy. Different collective terms have been used to bring such things together: in earlier ages, as we have said, they were variously called 'figures of speech' or 'tropes' (the latter implying a turning away from the normal functioning of particular words or idioms). It was often difficult to keep such tropes free of association with the very negative linguistic term 'cliché', as Pope suggests in the 'Essay on Criticism'. So the *Dictionary of Received Ideas* which Flaubert appended to his unfinished novel *Bouvard et Pécuchet* was copied in English by the Irish satirist Flann O'Brien as 'Catechism of Cliché'. The sliding of linguistic effects, which prize originality of impact above all else, into the predictability of cliché, is particularly undermining in poetry.

A good example of the operation of figurativeness is 'Corncrake', a short poem by Andrew McNeillie, which is a model of how metaphor works in conjunction with other poetic devices:

> Spring slips him in through a gap
> In a stone wall, a secret agent
> Bargaining with the underworld

> Against sleep, a bomb
> With a slow time-fuse, an old man
> Winding all our clocks on, and back.

If we had to assign this poem to a genre, we might say it is a riddle, like the riddles in the Anglo-Saxon *Exeter Book*. Without its title, we might puzzle over the poem's subject—who the 'him' in the first line refers to. But when we have the title, the poem is an astonishing rhapsody on the associations of this very secretive bird. Where they are still common, as on the island of Inishbofin off Connemara, their relentless craking in the early hours keeps people awake (as they did inland up to the 1950s). The slow time-fuse at the end suggests the bird's extinction in most parts of Britain and Ireland; the sound it makes has the relentless ticking of a clock, but its winding back suggests that we have to go to the past (and to the underworld, the realm of the dead) to find the bird now. And of course a bomb with a slow time-fuse has still to explode.

The poem shows how in the best poems metaphor does its work 'no pace perceived' (to borrow a metaphor from Shakespeare that perfectly expresses this quality), and how a poem can do several things at once. A prose description of the life and fate of the corncrake could not express those things more memorably than McNeillie's poem. The kind of riddle that this poem is has been prominent in English since Anglo-Saxon poetry: notably the collection of them in the great 11th-century manuscript ('*se micel bōc*': 'the large book') known as the *Exeter Book*. Even outside this collection, the poetic tendency in Old English has been called 'riddlic', because of its tendency to hold back the literal meaning. The most sophisticated and elusive system of such riddling is the form known as kenning in Old Norse, when things are expressed as compounds, neither element of which literally describes the thing itself: for example 'whale-road' for 'sea' in Old English (the sea is not a whale or a road).

Riddles bear an interesting relationship to figurative writing. If figuration describes things as what they are not literally, riddles describe things wholly literally as what they look like, without any attempt to interpret what they represent. Here is a particularly subtle, and brief, Anglo-Saxon riddle:

> I saw a woman sitting alone.

The translator of the riddle, Michael Alexander, recognized as the correct solution: 'A mirror'.

This bare observation gets its meaning by inviting a context in which the riddling first person 'I' means something that is worth remarking. The image in the Anglo-Saxon 'Ice' riddle is:

> There was a wonder on the road: water become bone.

As John Fuller shows in his book *Who is Ozymandias? And Other Puzzles in Poetry*, the riddling tendency is widely evident throughout the history of English poetry, from Anglo-Saxon to Shakespeare to Pope to Wallace Stevens. The form gained a new vitality, and a new name, 'Martian', in the 1970s with the publication of Craig Raine's collection *A Martian Sends a Postcard Home*, in which the title poem is a classic of defamiliarization in describing things as what they look like without giving the answer to the riddle: that is without saying what their significance or function is. Here is the poem's description of a telephone (in its older form):

> In homes, a haunted apparatus sleeps,
> that snores when you pick it up.
>
> If the ghost cries, they carry it
> to their lips and soothe it to sleep
>
> with sounds. And yet, they wake it up
> deliberately, by tickling with a finger.

Part of the subtlety here is the suppression of the word 'cradle' which can be applied either to a baby's bed or the holder of a telephone. Another poem in the book, 'Flying to Belfast, 1977', begins:

> It was possible to laugh
> as the engines whistled to the boil,
>
> and wonder what the clouds looked like—
> shovelled snow, Apple Charlotte.

What the riddling 'Martian' poet is wondering is: what can the clouds viewed from the plane be likened to?—rather as Dylan Thomas manages to express indirectly a truth about grief in his anomalous time-phrase 'a grief ago'.

The more we ponder it, the more central the practice of riddling—holding back meaning, or restoring the underlying meaning that the norms of observation have submerged—seems to the whole lyric impulse: not so much 'what oft was thought, but ne'er so well expressed' as what was waiting to be thought at all.

The sound of sense

A number of poets in the early 20th century were particularly interested in the centrality of sound in poetry. T. S. Eliot says, 'Poetry begins, I dare say, with a savage beating of a drum in a jungle, and it retains that essential of percussion and rhythm'. It is in this sense that the poet, Eliot says, can be said to be *older* than other human beings'. Osip Mandelstam's celebrated 'Conversation about Dante', described by Seamus Heaney as 'the greatest paean I know to the power which poetic imagination wields', sees physiological production as vital to Dante: the closeness of his phonetics to infant babbling and the dependence of the movement in both *Inferno* and *Purgatorio* on human gait and breathing. In listing the tropes and figures of speech, formal commentators have always emphasized the figures that relied on sound effects: alliteration and assonance where the patterned repetition of particular sounds—consonants or vowels—are essential to rhythm. A favoured device among the figures of speech is onomatopoeia, the linking of the sounds of words to their meaning. Some linguists have seen this phenomenon as fundamental to the whole operation of language, even constructing a methodology to represent it: for example, words in English ending in '-ump' tend to be associated with some kind of physical crudeness. Rhyme has an obvious role in organizing the structure of poetry on phonetic grounds.

One of the greatest exponents of sound effects in English poetry is Tennyson, in poems like 'Morte D'Arthur'. The passage describing Sir Bedivere after he has thrown the sword Excalibur into the lake is a celebrated example:

> Dry clash'd his harness in the icy caves
> And barren chasms, and all to left and right
> The bare black cliff clang'd round him, as he based
> His feet on juts of slippery crag that rang
> Sharp-smitten with the dint of armed heels—
> And on a sudden, lo! the level lake,
> And the long glories of the winter moon.

The ringing consonants and the alliteration of the 'barren chasms' and 'the bare black cliff clang'd' contrast musically with the long vowels of 'lo' and the 'glories of the winter moon', and are clearly an important part of the effectiveness of these stunning lines. Several poets throughout the 20th century—Frost, Ted Hughes, and Tom Paulin, for example—have emphasized such phonetic effects in their critical analyses, and there is no doubt that what Frost called 'the sound of sense' is a major intrinsic item in the poet's equipment. Indeed, its importance is a qualification of the insistence on the secondary status of verse form quoted from the authorities in the Introduction. But by 'the sound of sense'

Frost did not mean just the sonority of the words; he said that underlying linguistic usage was a more abstract 'sentence sound', which the speaker or poet had to be faithful to, and that 'the best place to get the abstract sound of sense is from voices behind a door that cuts off the words'.

Frost's sound of sense has something in common with what the late Victorian poet Gerard Manley Hopkins called 'sprung rhythm', which similarly claimed a connexion with normal speech. But as well as a theorist of rhythm, Hopkins was a virtuoso of poetic sonority:

> This darksome burn, horseback brown,
> His rollrock highroad roaring down,
> In coop and in comb the fleece of his foam
> Flutes and low to the lake falls home...
>
> Degged with dew, dappled with dew
> Are the groins of the braes that the brook treads through,
> Wiry heathpacks, flitches of fern,
> And the beadbonny ash that sits over the burn.

In fact the special devices Hopkins uses here are not only a matter of sound, prominent as that is. He invents expressive new compounds ('darksome', 'rollrock', 'heathpacks', 'beadbonny'), and uses words which are either localized ('burn', 'braes') or applied in surprising contexts ('horseback', 'highroad', 'coop and comb', 'groins', 'flitches'). Here, if anywhere, is a language that belongs particularly to poetry.

And, above all, Milton, Tennyson's 'mighty-mouthed inventor of harmonies', is the great master of sounding poetry in English.

> Him the almighty power
> Hurled headlong flaming from the ethereal sky
> With hideous ruin and combustion down

> To bottomless perdition, there to dwell
> In adamantine chains and penal fire,
> Who durst defy the omnipotent to arms.

Modern dictionary definitions of poetry tend to use the term 'rhythm' more insistently than anything else, and, though that word can be applied to patterning generally, its primary application is to sound. No feature of the poetic is less dispensable than the sound of sense that Frost identified.

However, it should be noted that not all commentators have accepted the view that in poetry sound is an end in itself. In a vigorous attack on what he calls 'Suggestion Theory'—the idea that since the Romantics something less definable than 'Meaning' has had primacy in poetry—Bateson in *English Poetry: A Critical Introduction*, takes issue too with what he calls 'The Pure Sound Theory'. According to this theory, Poe for example claimed that 'Nevermore' was the refrain-word in his poem 'The Raven' because 'the long *o* is the most sonorous vowel'. Early in the 20th century the idea of poetry as pure sound was developed with great force: in 'The Manifesto' of imagism, Ezra Pound and F. S. Flint urged: 'Study "cadences", the finest that you can discover, preferably in a foreign language so that the meaning of the words may be less likely to divert your attention from the movement. Saxon charms, Hebridean folk-songs, Dante, and the lyrics of Goethe and Shakespeare (apart from their meaning) are especially recommended.' The rationalist Bateson says, 'It is odd that this kind of thing can ever have been taken seriously'. Never the less, it has been a recurrent inclination in poetics to see poetry as defined importantly by its sound. Ted Hughes invented a sound-language called Orghast for his version of the myth of Prometheus. Frost's suggestive phrase suggests admirably the way that sound carries much of the weight of what is most indispensable in poetry.

Chapter 4
The kinds of poetry and their contexts

Shakespeare's scepticism about the naming of dramatic genres is indicated by his assigning to the tedious and overcircumstantial Polonius the task of itemizing them: 'The best actors in the world, either for tragedy, comedy, history, pastoral, pastoral-comical, historical-pastoral, tragical-historical, tragical-comical-historical-pastoral, scene individable, or poem unlimited.' The sections of this chapter illustrate the difficulty with the genres of poetry. Having considered what characteristics may be thought definitive of poetry—rhythmic form, or ritual, or distinctive language, and the question of moral and political seriousness and intelligibility—we might go on to this chimerical task of considering the subsections into which poetry as a whole can be, and has been, divided.

Many different things have been described as poetry—different ways of writing; ways of seeing the world; states of mind. But, to begin with, in the Western tradition there are three established structural categories of writing that come under the heading of poetry. Principally, since the Greeks (notably in Plato's *Republic*), these have been defined as epic, drama, and lyric. Each of these tends to be dominant in different periods and each has its characteristic strengths; proponents of each feel that their kind is of crucial importance, often relegating the significance of the other two. We are rather blind nowadays to these varying categorical claims because the lyric is so much in the ascendant in definitions and theories of poetry. Abrams dates this dominance back to the early 19th century: to Wordsworth, who thought of the lyrical poem, rather than epic or tragedy, as the exemplary form. Francis Jeffrey, in 'The State of Modern Poetry', conceded that among contemporary poets 'short pieces…are frequently very delightful' but that 'we have not wings, it would seem, for a long flight': something that seems to be even more true in the post-Romantic age.

There were earlier periods when the lyric seemed to be similarly dominant. But there were ages too when the lyric shared its dominance with other forms: the German love poets of the Middle Ages, the *Minnesänger*, composed both epic love poems and lyrics. The composer of *Parsifal*, Wolfram von Eschenbach, wrote some of the finest love lyrics of the European tradition. In turning to the Middle Ages, Richard Wagner, as well as drawing on Germanic epics for his great music-dramas, also composed an opera, *The Mastersingers of Nuremberg*, about the composers of love lyrics.

The most familiar case in English of a writer of lyric and longer works is of course Shakespeare himself, whose plays contain some of the greatest lyric poetry in English and whose sonnets are some of the most prized short poems in the language. In his time, tragedy, comedy, and the sonnet seemed to be equally amenable to effective poetic expression. Just as Sidney and the Romantics found poetry of the highest kind expressed in prose, so some of Shakespeare's most memorable poetry comes in the plays, such as Perdita's beautiful flower-lists in *The Winter's Tale*:

> O Proserpina,
> For the flowers now that, frighted, thou lett'st fall
> From Dis's waggon!—daffodils,
> That come before the swallow dares, and take
> The winds of March with beauty; violets dim,

But sweeter than the lids of Juno's eyes
Or Cytherea's breath; pale primroses,
That die unmarried ere they can behold
Bright Phoebus in his strength,—a malady
Most incident to maids.

In a series of essays throughout his life, T. S. Eliot returned obsessively to the question of 'The Possibility of a Poetic Drama', the title of one of those essays, ending with a longer consideration of 'Poetry and Drama' in 1951 in which he explains why his own attempts at poetic drama are unsuccessful in various ways. Ironically in the light of the several plays Eliot wrote in the form, nobody argues the impossibility of such drama in the modern age so convincingly. Why was drama in verse possible in the Elizabethan and Jacobean era but not in the 20th century (nor indeed in the time of the great Romantic lyricists who also attempted to write poetic dramas without conspicuous success, as Eliot says: Shelley, for instance, whose poetic dramas are in general seen as even less successful than Eliot's)?

If the same effects of poetry can occur in the lyric and in drama, as in *The Winter's Tale*, it would seem that there is nothing in the *linguistic* nature of poetry that belongs exclusively to one genre or the other. It is easy to think of celebrated extracts from the works of Elizabethan and Jacobean playwrights which manifest lyric compression: 'Cover her face. Mine eyes dazzle. She died young'; 'Her lips suck forth my soul: see where it flies!'; 'Tomorrow and tomorrow and tomorrow | Creeps in this petty pace from day to day'; 'Oh my oblivion is a very Antony | And I am all forgotten'; 'Keep up your bright swords; for the dew will rust them.'

Lyric effects also occur in the epic. An obvious shared case is the Homeric simile: whatever the rationale is for the simple one-for-one correspondence in the single simile and metaphor considered earlier here, its development in the epic turns it into the kind of image in motion that Lessing was concerned with in 'Laocoon'.

F. R. Leavis called the similes in *Paradise Lost* 'smuggled-in pieces of imaginative indulgence', quoting the glorious and extravagant Homeric simile for Satan's travels in book III of *Paradise Lost*:

> As when a vulture on Imaus bred,
> Whose snowy ridge the roving Tartar bounds,
> Dislodging from a region scarce of prey
> To gorge the flesh of lambs or yeanling kids
> On hills where flocks are fed, flies towards the springs
> Of Ganges or Hydaspes, Indian streams;
> But in his way lights on the barren plains
> Of Sericana, where Chineses drive
> With sails and wind their cany waggons light:
> So on this windy sea of land, the fiend
> Walked up and down alone, bent on his prey.

Folded within the developed parallel of Satan with the threatening vulture, the miniature of the Chinese figures driving their cane waggons is a momentary image that might seem to reduce the perspective by use of a shorter but picturesque form (as does Chaucer's 'smiler with the knife under the cloak' in the long romance of *The Knight's Tale*).

I am aware of the apparent paradox of stressing from the start the grandest claim—Shelley's—that is made for the poets as the legislators of the world, and then failing to deal much with epic, the grandest form of poetry. Clearly, lyrical appeal is a feature of writers of epic scope in modern writers as well as Milton. Derek Walcott's *Omeros* is an extraordinary epic of West Indian life, named after the Greek term for Homer and aspiring to the historical scope of Homeric epic. Within that scope, Walcott writes with a lyricism more associated with the lyric:

> Under the thick leaves of the forest, there's a life
> more intricate than ours, with our vows of love,
> that seethes under the spider's veil on the wet leaf.

The material of Homer's epics also informs one of Walcott's most celebrated lyric poems, 'Sea Grapes':

> That sail which leans on light,
>
> tired of islands,
> a schooner beating up the Caribbean
>
> for home, could be Odysseus,
> home-bound on the Aegean.

Similarly, the Irish poet Eiléan Ní Chuilleanáin's admired lyric 'The Second Voyage' begins with Odysseus resting on his oar. The epic and the lyric have a symbiotic existence in language.

Of the Greek categories, the role of the epic itself has largely been taken over by the novel which is often concerned with the fates of societies and peoples as the epic was; the novel has similarly taken over the role of the romance, the dominant narrative form in the medieval and Renaissance periods. The dramatic is now regarded as a separate category altogether: insofar as it relates to poetry, the poetic is thought to be an element within the dramatic. Thus in his crucial *Poetics* discussion of how the poet handles plot (in the epic and the drama) Aristotle says that plot and character can occur in both verse and prose. Because the short poem is so much in the ascendant since the Romantics the *Poetics* discussion seems to us hardly to come under poetry at all, primarily concerned as it is with tragedy and to a lesser extent comedy; lyric only occurs as one of six subservient features of dramatic works.

Still, it would be strange to begin a modern account of poetic genres nowadays with anything other than lyric. The dominance of the lyric form is a large aesthetic question, the resolution of which would take us beyond the margins of poetry into more wide-ranging considerations of ethics and aesthetics (and maybe attention spans). I want to turn next to some various fields in which the lyric has been dominant, and some of the generic changes that have come about through its dominance.

A fundamental factor of the lyric of course is length. In considering the various matters of definition that poetry raises, one of the most surprising (though it is one that we are too familiar with to remark it much) is the question of size. It is curious that the same term, 'poem', is used to describe *Paradise Lost* and Milton's sonnet 'On His Blindness'—rather as if the same categorical term were used to describe *War and Peace* and a Raymond Carver short story. Certainly there are subsections of the poem in terms of genre: *Paradise Lost* is an epic while 'On His Blindness' is—what? To say it is a sonnet is to give a different kind of answer generically.

There are many such awkward cases: long poems which have shorter poems as components of them. For example, if Tennyson's *Idylls of the King* is thought of as a single poem, what exactly is the 'Morte D'Arthur'? If Eliot's *Four Quartets* is a single poem, what is 'Little Gidding' within it? It is certainly more substantial than other poems that are regarded as complete works. To put it in the most pedantic terms, there are poems where the commentator has to pause before deciding whether to italicize a title as the name of a whole work, or to leave it in quotation-marks as the title of a single poem. Yeats's volume called *The Tower* contains a single poem called 'The Tower'.

This doesn't matter crucially to the wider question of deciding what a poem is. But there seem to be poems that are too long or multifaceted to think of them as a single poem, and there are poems that seem too short to think of them as a poem. Keats's 'This Living Hand' is categorized as a fragment, though at seven-and-a-half lines it is longer than some poems. It is perhaps thought to be fragmentary because it ends with a half-line: many poets did that in the 20th century and since, but not Keats in his completed poems. More particularly, it is a roughly written draft on the back of a more formal piece of writing.

Commonly cited as a challenging short poem, though it is never denied the status of poem, is Ezra Pound's 'In a Station of the

Metro', discussed already. Clearly these two lines are protected by the presence of a substantial authorial title: one of the constructs that establish a poem's claim. In Pound's modernist era, the emergence of the sequence poem was a significant development, supplanting the longer Victorian narrative. Though there were Victorian sequences like Tennyson's *Idylls of the King* which brought together poems on linked themes, in the modernist sequences what seem to be quite distinct individual poems are gathered together under a single title, as in Eliot's 'The Waste Land'.

Pastoral, public poetry, and satire

Although the categories of epic, drama, and lyric have particular dominance, in the Western tradition since the classics other generic terms are encountered. A clear example is the pastoral which, among the recognized traditional genres, has retained a surprising resilience.

The tendency of pastoral to combine artificiality with political explicitness has been commented on, from Virgil to Edmund Spenser. When Virgil wanted to comment more or less expressly on the public circumstances of his time, he did it not through epic or a recognized political form, but in his *Eclogues*. When Spenser wanted to write on the Protestant conquest of Munster in the Elizabethan era, his spokesmen were the fictitious shepherds like Colin Clout and his friends, and the venerated queen was Cynthia. But he described the local rivers and towns in County Cork, and their names, with striking accuracy, in the same way that the Jamaican poet Lorna Goodison's poem 'To Us All Flowers Are Roses' is a convincing, unapologetic use of place names expected to be unfamiliar.

The pastoral typically combines geographical accuracy with artificial settings. Perhaps what seems the least political of forms, with its 'nymphs and shepherds', can represent the political precisely because it seems free of ideological designs. So it enables the development of political or national poetry—an idea which seems oddly opposed to the universality with which we started.

The arguments about national and political poetry through history are highly contradictory. Poetry is faced with a dilemma: it is obliged to descend from its ivory tower to take the public world seriously, but it must avoid the charge of jingoism and of being co-opted in a particular political cause. In his *Essay on Dramatic Poesy*, Dryden's Crites, 'a person of a sharp judgment' whom we heard from in the Introduction, fears that the defeat of the Dutch in the Medway will inspire triumphalism in 'those eternal Rhymers, who watch a battle with more diligence than the Ravens and birds of Prey'. He reflects gloomily on the form that political poetry tends to take, saying 'he could scarce have wished the Victory at the price he knew he must pay for it, in being subject to the reading and hearing of so many ill verses as he was sure would be made upon it'.

It is often suggested nowadays too that poets not only cannot but should not be involved in any kind of public debate, whatever Shelleyan claims are made for their role as unacknowledged legislators. In an early spoof poem, 'Lunch with Pancho Villa', the Northern Irish poet Paul Muldoon discusses the matter with mock earnestness: the poem's politically engaged speaker, Pancho Villa, says:

> 'Look, son. Just look around you.
> People are getting themselves killed
> Left, right and centre
> While you do what? Write rondeaux?
> There's more to living in this country
> Than stars and horses, pigs and trees,
> Not that you'd guess it from your poems.
> Do you never listen to the news?
> You want to get down to something true,
> Something a little nearer home.'

We get the grim joke, and we hear again the voice of Peacock objecting to Coleridge's 'gewgaws', in the ascribed attitude here. By the end of the poem, this speaker anticipates gloomily his conversation with this 'callow youth | who learned to write last winter— | one of those correspondence courses', expecting that

> He'll be rambling on, no doubt,
> About pigs and trees, stars and horses.

And it seems he'll be right; in general Muldoon—or the poem's fictional 'callow youth'—takes the view that pigs, trees, and the like (the age-old standbys of nature as a central topic for poetry) are a more appropriate subject for it than the news and the politics of the country, especially if that country is Northern Ireland of the 1970s with its fraught and murderous politics.

No doubt that is one implication here: a contrast between nature poetry and poetry of more public significance. We might pause though to ask what exactly is being offered as the alternative to writing about public affairs: stars and horses, pigs and trees, wind and snow, flowers and herbs. They are the everyday observed things of nature, certainly—things which we have seen are a favourite poetic field. Muldoon's list is strikingly similar to the 'birds, beasts, herbs, and trees' of Confucius in the *Analects*. The critic Po Chu-I of the Six Dynasties criticized the poets of the period for their ornate style and for writing on such themes as 'wind and snow, flowers and herbs' without using them for allegorical purposes. The list recalls too the 'mountains and rivers' of American poets of the wilds such as Gary Snyder who drew on the subjects of Tao (Zen): people who have any acquaintance with poetry recognize these lists as standard materials of poetry. But they are things of more moment too. Stars are what we see in the sky, the objects of sense perception just as the other items in the list are; but they are also the subject of the writings of Hesiod at the origins of Greek mythological poetry. About stars in that sense we have no first-hand knowledge at all. There are further mythological associations: horses might include Pegasus, the winged steed of poetry; and from Eden to the world-tree of Old Norse, trees have a central place.

One way of reading Muldoon's poem is to see it as a claim that serious poetry can if it likes be about nature, and nothing more. But if we do derive such a moral here, it is a claim that is far from universal in the discussion of poetry, either in time or place. The speaker of Muldoon's fiction is the revolutionary Mexican leader Pancho Villa who was assassinated in 1923 and is remembered as a folk hero because of his demands for the alleviation of poverty—the hero too of a celebrated war documentary silent film from 1912. And some 20th-century poets and critics, particularly in the aftermath of the horrors of the Holocaust and World War II, might be enlisted to side with Muldoon's Pancho Villa against the callow youth, in demanding more attention to serious matters.

The matter of poetry's public obligations is an ageless debate, from ancient Chinese, to the medieval troubadours, and on to the Romantics like Shelley and Byron. It involves Plato's famous reservation about poets' failure to trade in realities, one of the principal grounds on which he excluded them from the *Republic*. But, even if it is conceded that poetry has the right, if not even the obligation, to pronounce on public matters, it has generally been thought that it is difficult to write political poetry well.

A strikingly successful application of poetic effects to a public situation was the appearance of Michael Longley's poem 'Ceasefire' in the *Irish Times* in the week that the first ceasefire was signed in Northern Ireland in 1994. Longley's poem is a classic employment of literary allusion: the poem tells of the meeting of Priam and Achilles after the fall of Troy, ending with Priam getting down on his knees to 'kiss Achilles' hand, the killer of my son'. The title refers to the current Irish situation with delicacy and tact, like pastoral, free of political judgement.

One problem with discussion of particular political issues in poetry, rather than wider matters of public ethics, is that political judgements and ideology change from age to age. For example, the first edition of Palgrave's *Golden Treasury* in 1861 contained the extraordinarily racist and chauvinistic 'The Private of the Buffs' by Sir F. H. Doyle (it survived in all editions up to 1926):

> Yes, Honour calls!—with strength like steel
> He puts the vision by.
> Let dusky Indians whine and kneel;
> An English lad must die.

Clearly the high-minded obligation of poetry to deal with the external world and to descend to 'impure poetry' has risks. A subcategory often used in anthologies was 'occasional verse', poetry written to mark a particular occasion, personal or public. Giorgos Seferis and several poets after him in the 20th century made a claim that seems strange at first hearing: that 'poetry can help'. Yeats coined a magnificent phrase to describe artistic attempts to cope with political difficulties, referring to the Irish Civil War of the 1920s: art must provide 'befitting emblems of adversity', a term which his Irish follower Heaney echoed and rephrased as finding expressions 'adequate to our predicament'.

As well as pastoral, there are other categories of uncertain definition that we encounter looking through anthologies of poetry. The most important of these is satire (there are others, such as the 'Odes' of Keats), which is particularly unsettling because nowadays we have strong, particular associations with it, as negative criticism. The word 'satire' is descended from the Latin term 'satura', a general term for poetic mixture, and this is the loose sense in which it applies to the poems by Donne (and others) called satires. The category in Horace refers to such general reflection on the nature of human happiness and literary success, with none of the negative connotations the term has for us; our sense has more connection with the satires of Juvenal which are similarly concerned with general truth and observation but with those critical overtones. Juvenal was the model for the 18th-century English satirists, including Samuel Johnson whose poems 'London' and 'The Vanity of Human Wishes' are drawn from him. Johnson's Juvenalian lines on the Swedish King Gustavus Adolphus are much quoted:

> His fall was destined to a barren strand
> A petty fortress, and a dubious hand.
> He left the name at which the world grew pale
> To point a moral or adorn a tale.

In the same way that poetic style often depends on explicit, established linguistic rules to depart from them, satire relies on some general truth, some understood order of things to be followed or departed from. Like the pastoral, it is a classical form which has an important history in English poetry; it shares its distribution both with prose fiction and with popular media. Its relationship with political norms is a fraught one; broadly speaking, since Juvenal it has been a conservative form because of its dependence on shared norms of understanding. Though there were significant predecessors in the Middle Ages in English (writers like John Skelton and William Dunbar, and to some extent Geoffrey Chaucer), the great age of satire in English poetry was the Augustan period, with the classical revival at the end of the 17th and into the 18th century. The great political satirists in poetry were Dryden and Pope. Dryden's 'Absalom and Achitophel' satirizes public figures in a way that might be thought daring in the media satires of our age, as in these lines on the Duke of Buckingham:

> Some of their chiefs were princes of the land:
> In the first rank of these did Zimri stand,

> A man so various that he seemed to be
> Not one but all mankind's epitome:
> Stiff in opinions, always in the wrong,
> Was everything by starts, and nothing long,
> But, in the course of one revolving moon,
> Was chemist, fiddler, statesman and buffoon...

In 'A Discourse Concerning the Original and Progress of Satire', Dryden says, 'The nicest and most delicate touches of satire consist in fine raillery... How easy it is to call rogue and villain, and that wittily? But how hard to make a man appear a fool, a blockhead, or a knave, without using any of those opprobrious terms.' And he goes on to say that the original of Zimri (without naming Buckingham) 'was too witty to resent it as an injury'. Dryden is opposed to the kind of invective—personalized satire—of the age, and declares a preference for Horace over Juvenal. In any case, satire is clearly an important way that poetry can be political, even if it cannot in Auden's terms make things happen. In the same way that epic has been taken over by the novel, satire in our time is less associated with poetry than with journalistic prose, while there is a clear tradition extending from Hogarth and Gillray to vigorous cartoon invectivists like Steve Bell.

Popular poetry and universal appeal

Whether or not poetry is concerned with public issues, its expression varies in the directness or otherwise of its language. We looked in Chapter 3 at places where poetry achieves its effects by employing language in an unusual way: perhaps in a way that is found exhilarating by the reader of poetry, but still an unusual way. If there is such a language reserved for poetry to any extent, does this linguistic exclusiveness account for poetry's failure to achieve widespread popularity? Is it a factor in Adrian Mitchell's widely quoted accusation, set at the head of his *Poems 1953–2008*?

> Most people ignore most poetry
> because
> most poetry ignores most people.

This is a matter of subject: most people, it seems to say, are not the subject of most poetry. Perhaps the specialized language of poetry is part of the problem. But it is also a question of audience: who are poetic voices addressing themselves to? It raises the question too of who it is that poetry as a whole is addressed to. It was all very well—and important—for Mitchell to complain that poetry ignores most people. But have 'most people' *really* expressed the wish that poetry should address itself to them? The genial American poet-satirist Billy Collins reminds us that 'one of the ridiculous aspects of being a poet is the huge gulf between how seriously we take ourselves and how generally we are ignored by everybody else'.

There are kinds of entertainment (if that is what poetry is) that are popular with 'most people', especially—and by definition—popular music. Here, once again, we have to be aware of the context that writing and songs occur in: some contexts are more hospitable to poetry than others. Everyone is aware of the general appeal of popular songs: the kind of thing called by Noël Coward 'the power of cheap music'. Can poetry compete? Or does it have some kind of appeal to taste or judgement that means it is fated from the start to be the concern of an élite?

There are poems that have some general popularity: a kind of poetry that is not necessarily concerned either with political issues or with birds and flowers or with 'most people', but which, unlike Mitchell's 'most poetry', *does* seem to prompt a response in most of those who read it. Mostly this is narrative poetry which performs a function more usually associated nowadays with prose (which through the short story has tended to take over the role

of the longish narrative poem that was so successful in the
19th century for poets like Scott, Tennyson, Browning, and Christina
Rossetti). In English, everyone who encounters it responds to the
opening of Scott's 'The Lady of the Lake':

> The stag at eve had drunk his fill
> Where danced the moon on Monan's rill,
> And deep his midnight lair had made
> In lone Glenartney's hazel shade.

The appeal of Scott's opening seems to be the sound of the lines
(I will touch later on the evocativeness of place names in
considering sound in poetry); the poem has no more to do with
the lives of 'most people' than any of the poems that Mitchell says
ignore them. It is easy to think of other examples of this 'popular
reciter' type: Byron's 'The Assyrian came down like a wolf on the
fold'; or the compelling Gothic narrative of Gibson's eerie 'Flannan
Isle'; or Alfred Noyes's 'The Highwayman', once voted as the nation's
favourite poem.

Modern movements like rap or 'spoken word' poetry could be
seen partly as a calculated attempt to switch into this receptive
world; a poet like Grace Nichols uses rap side by side with her
powerful feminist statement poems such as 'I is a Long-Memoried
Woman'. In the 20th century the longer narrative poems by the
Canadian Robert Service had real popularity; 'Dangerous Dan
McGrew' and 'The Cremation of Sam Magee' were common
party-pieces in public house gatherings. So were the Australian
Irish poems by Father Patrick Joseph Hartigan, 'John O'Brien',
Around the Boree Log.

But I don't think it is necessary to shift into quite so different a
kind of writing and/or performance to find poems that have
universal appeal. Yeats's 'The Lake Isle of Innisfree' is probably
such a poem, with its 'lake-water lapping' that the poet says he

3. 'The Lake Isle of Innisfree.'

hears 'in the deep heart's core' (see Figure 3). There was an interesting piece of evidence that general popularity need not depend on anthologized familiarity when 'the nation' voted through the BBC for a contemporary poem, Jenny Joseph's 'Warning', which begins 'When I am an old woman I shall wear purple | With a red hat which doesn't go', as its favourite poem. What exactly, we wonder, was the universal note that Joseph struck there? Is it what has been called 'yes poetry': something which finds an answering echo in every breast? It is also funny: something else to be dealt with as a distinct genre later in this chapter.

No doubt different qualities account for the popularity of these different poems: 'The Lady of the Lake' holds the reader by the interest of its narrative as well as by its rhythmical drive, while Joseph's poem has general appeal because (like Philip Larkin's 'Aubade') it *does* reflect general sentiments. It is poetry that for once doesn't ignore most people, and it cheerfully celebrates the power to be outrageous, and to avoid the self-regard that is often associated with poetry.

Despite his attack on generalizations, no poem in English better captures this note of universality than Blake's 'The Mental Traveller', or his 'Auguries of Innocence':

> A Robin Red breast in a Cage
> Puts all Heaven in a Rage...
> A Horse mis'usd upon the Road
> Calls to Heaven for Human blood...
> He who shall hurt the little Wren
> Shall never be belov'd by Men...
> A truth that's told with bad intent
> Beats all the lies you can invent...
> The poor Man's Farthing is worth more
> Than all the Gold on Afric's Shore...
> The Harlot's cry from Street to Street
> Shall weave Old England's winding Sheet...
> Every Night & every Morn
> Some to Misery are Born.

Nothing in English poetry answers Mitchell's complaint on behalf of 'most people' better than this: it is a way of describing experience which it seems to be recognized that poetry copes with best, in the face of the great emotions: here social justice, but notably love and death and bereavement. Poetry is perhaps closest to prayer in this capacity. Laurence Binyon's lines from 'For the Fallen' are readily accessible; but it is interesting to ponder whether they would have had the same impact if they did not employ the liturgical-sounding inversion of normal syntax: the stately 'They shall grow not old', rather than the usual 'They shall not grow old'. Binyon's line, like Cory's 'Heraclitus' considered later, remains general but somehow seems to have the collective force of all the individuals who died or who survived. Perhaps it is that quality which prompted Geoffrey Hill to call his first collection *For the Unfallen*: general truths about the living to correspond to those about the dead.

In the cases of Blake and Yeats as poets of general appeal there is the same irony as in the extreme case of James Joyce (often claimed as the Irish people's novelist but described in a song by Terry Eagleton as 'the greatest Irish genius that nobody can read'). Many of Blake's writings are baffling and esoteric, despite the universal appeal of passages like the lines quoted from 'Auguries of Innocence'. It is curious that the best 'popular reciter' poets such as Blake and Yeats are sometimes also writers of the most obscure poetry. This apparent paradox also leads on to another rather disconcerting question: are the things that people like about poetry (when they do like it) the same things that entitle poetry to the high estimation we hear claimed for it?

Poetry of place

Among the kinds of poetry that seem to win something like universal popularity, as well as the expression of universal sentiment comes what has been called in an increasingly recurrent mantra, 'poetry of place'. Why exactly does everyone who knows it like Edward Thomas's 'Adlestrop'? It is partly of course that the poem has another variety of universality as a quintessence of English pastoralism: all the more poignant, written in 1915, for its setting in that pre-war juncture, in the year from which Larkin named another crucial poem, 'MCMXIV' (with its devastating, pre-war last line: 'Never such innocence again').

As well as the universality of the events, in both cases the particular references contribute to the evocativeness: is it partly the repetition in Thomas's last lines—'Farther and farther, all the birds | Of Oxfordshire and Gloucestershire'—that stirs all readers? No doubt the fact that the event the poem commemorates is resonant—the unscheduled stopping of a train at a quiet Gloucestershire station in June 1914, just before the outbreak of the war in which Thomas was to die. This very particular moment is, quietly, combined with the universality of normal experience: 'The steam hissed. Someone cleared his throat.'

This unostentatious line echoes down the 20th century in English poetry—for example, turning to Larkin again, in another train poem which is both like and unlike 'Adlestrop', 'Whitsun Weddings', with its similarly universal evocation of English summer train-travel:

> an Odeon, a cooling-tower,
> and someone running up to bowl.

But to suggest that there is something else operating here, more than English pastoral, we might note a common feature in several of these passages: the occurrence in them of the formal names of things and places or other kinds of special vocabulary: Monan's rill, Glenartney, Oxfordshire and Gloucestershire, an Odeon. Patrick Kavanagh made a celebrated distinction between what he called the parochial and the provincial. Parochial writing—emanating from the home parish—simply represents that parish without any sense of an authoritative centre that it is cut off from. Provincial writers think of themselves as being distant from the significant centre where the literary action is. The use of place names (like Kavanagh's own Gortin or Inishkeen) has a reassuring air of integrity in writing about a real place, known to the writer.

In these usages—the parochial, or the use of place names and proper nouns—we are once again dealing with words that are not part of the normal, general vocabulary of the language. We might reflect slightly further on what were called by Latin grammarians 'proper nouns': that is, nouns that have a particular rather than a general denotation. They may then be in the same category as words and images we have noted already as out of the ordinary in diction: the 'ground agast', rose-leaves like burning coals on the water. In 'Whitsun Weddings', Larkin's placing of the indefinite article before 'Odeon' plays neatly with this device. 'Odeon' ought to be a proper noun, as its capital suggests. But the fact that it is a common cinema name means that it also functions as a common noun, if not quite common enough to write it as 'odeon' without the capital letter of the proper noun. In his chapter on 'Originality' in *The Work of Poetry*, one of the most compelling modern analyses of poetry and poetics, John Hollander reminds us that from Plato's *Cratylus* and *The Book of Genesis* to Emerson and Nietzsche in the 19th century, the power of assigning names has been seen as the primary creative operation of poetry and creativity in general.

It seems that we are finding again here a paradox about the popularity of poems which are popular. They seem to be either simple and immediately intelligible (like 'The stag at eve') or obscure ('Quinquireme of Nineveh from distant Ophir', the start of John Masefield's 'Cargoes'): the favourite pieces need not be 'simple' poems (or 'verse') and may be in a kind of language we don't have to comprehend fully or even quite accurately. And the places referred to don't need to be familiar. What has been called 'Yes poetry' in relation to details like Jenny Joseph's hat is popular because it chimes with the experience of the reader or hearer. But the category of popular poems we have just been considering—the place names and the proper nouns—seem to have an appeal precisely through unfamiliarity: Glenartney or Gortin or Dromahair.

A famous popular example is the start of Macaulay's 'Horatius'—'Lars Porsena of Clusium, | By the nine gods he swore'—which doesn't really invite us to ponder where Clusium is. No doubt sound effects contribute to this kind of appeal, a category which has been included in anthologies of popular verse; and again, it is a major element in the power of Milton, the mighty-mouthed inventor of harmonies: Satan,

> Lay floating many a rood, in bulk as huge
> As whom the fables name of monstrous size,
> Titanian, or Earth-born, that warred on Jove,
> Briareos or Typhon, whom the den
> By ancient Tarsus held, or that sea-beast
> Leviathan, which God of all his works
> Created hugest that swim the ocean stream.

Our ignorance of the names here does not detain us; their epic sonorities are reinforced by their unfamiliarity. Milton is the greatest naming poet in English, especially in the first two books of *Paradise Lost* where the places named belong to the exotic real world and to the world of legend and literature.

Comic and nonsense verse, and regularity

A clear case of popular poetry is what has been called comic verse, sometimes reductively. Like the examples we have been looking at, this tends to rely on formal regularity, especially rhyme. Popular comic verse is mostly directed, at least ostensibly, at children, by writers such as A. A. Milne, Hilaire Belloc, or Roald Dahl. But in periods like the Augustan age, when regularity of poetic form was in the ascendant, poets like Pope used comic forms in contexts which are not directed at children:

> I am his Highness' dog at *Kew*.
> Pray tell me Sir, whose Dog are you?

Or Pope's satirical lines on book 4 of *Gulliver's Travels*, when Gulliver's wife discovers his preference for horses over people:

> Forth in the street I rush with frantic cries;
> The windows open, all the neighbours rise:

'Where sleeps my Gulliver? O tell me where.'
The neighbours answer, 'With the sorrel mare.'

There was a return to such comic regularity by some writers in
the 20th century, notably by James Fenton in poems such as
'God: A Poem', which manifests many of the technical strengths
of English poetry—Chaucerian play on register from colloquial
to learned based on variety of linguistic origin; punning; metrical
and rhyming technique:

> 'I didn't exist at Creation,
> I didn't exist at the Flood,
> And I won't be around for Salvation
> To sort out the sheep from the cud—
>
> Or whatever the phrase is. The fact is
> In soteriological terms
> I'm a crude existential malpractice
> And you are a diet of worms.
>
> You're a nasty surprise in a sandwich.
> You're a drawing-pin caught in my sock.
> You're the limpest of shakes from a hand which
> I'd have thought would be firm as a rock.'

This illustrates brilliantly the general principle that demanding
poetic forms are particularly suited to what is called light verse.
Another modern master is Roald Dahl whose *Revolting Rhymes*
rewrite fairy stories for the modern age in a language that is
suitable for children but also has a receiving adult audience in
mind. For example, his Snow White appeared in 1982, after a
period of widespread reflection on the marital plans of the Prince
of Wales. The poem comments on the death of Snow White's
mother when her father the King must seek a new wife:

> It's never easy for a king
> To find himself that sort of thing.

The adult reading to a child will get the reference, over the child's head.

A related category of lyric that uses demanding forms unseriously is nonsense verse where there is no accumulation of meaning at all. The most noted exponents in English are Edward Lear and Lewis Carroll (though there is some overlap with the surreal verse of writers such as William Carlos Williams). What this kind of writing does is to fulfil the grammatical rules of the language but not the norms of vocabulary (a striking parallel is the writing of James Joyce in his two major works: in *Ulysses* the individual words are well formed but grammar is frequently breached; in *Finnegans Wake* the words are malformed but organized into normal syntax). The classic case in English is Carroll's 'Jabberwocky' in *Through the Looking-Glass*:

> 'Twas brillig, and the slithy toves
> Did gyre and gimble in the wabe:
> All mimsy were the borogroves;
> And the mome raths outgrabe.

In an incisive piece of poetry criticism, Alice says: 'It seems very pretty...but it's rather hard to understand...Somehow it seems to fill my head with ideas—only I don't know exactly what they are! However, somebody killed something: that's clear at any rate' (see Figure 4). The condition Alice describes is familiar in a period when there was a fashion for the notion of poetry that communicates before it is understood. It is the appeal of accomplished formalists like A. A. Milne who similarly mixes the immediately intelligible with the unfamiliar—in this case an improbable bit of naming:

> James James
> Morrison Morrison
> Wetherby George Dupree
> Took great

care of his mother
Though he was only three.

4. John Tenniel, illustration to Lewis Carroll's 'Jabberwocky', 1871.

Elegy, consolation, wisdom poetry, and therapy

However, if comic and nonsense verse often depend for their effectiveness on formal regularity, it is clear that regularity of form can also serve higher purposes. Among the typical fields of expertise proposed for poetry, Auden, and others, emphasize poetry's connection with death and the dead; Czesław Miłosz said, 'The living owe it to those who no longer can speak to tell their story for them' in poetry. Auden's view that poetry is a means of communicating with the dead has a long classical heritage: and of course elegy is one of the major genres.

People who never feel prompted to reflect on the nature of poetry often find it has a function and meaning for them, in offering some kind of comfort or consolation. In recent times, the lyric has found particular favour for the expression of personal emotion. In the 20th century the American poet Robert Lowell wrote a kind of poetry drawing on the materials of the poet's own life, which was termed 'confessional', exploiting the use of the first person which has always been prominent in the lyric. This application of poetry (we might recall the term 'use' in the title of T. S. Eliot's book *The Use of Poetry and the Use of Criticism*) is particularly often invoked in contemporary discussion, though the idea of artistic 'consolation' has never lapsed since Boethius's *Consolation of Philosophy* in the 5th century. It is particularly prominent and successful in the Old English poems called 'elegies' (for which indeed 'consolations' might be a better term).

In its ability to console, poetry is perhaps close to prayer in this capacity. The most familiar case in English is Binyon's 'For the Fallen': 'They shall grow not old, as we that are left grow old', which has attained a kind of liturgical status. As in this case, the best known poems are not necessarily by the best known poets: one of the most cherished English elegies, canonized by its inclusion in Quiller-Couch's *Oxford Book of English Verse*, is a translation by the Victorian Eton schoolmaster William Johnson Cory of a Greek elegy by Callimachus:

> They told me, Heraclitus, they told me you were dead.
> They brought me bitter news to hear and bitter tears to shed.
> I wept as I remember'd how often you and I
> Had tired the sun with talking and sent him down the sky.

To account for the effectiveness of such anthology pieces some such idea as 'the unchanging human heart' has been evoked. When the Australian cricketer Phillip Hughes died tragically in late 2014, this poem was read with huge impact at his funeral, to an audience that I suppose mostly didn't know—or care—who Heraclitus (or Cory) was.

A good example of a strict regular form which has been put to a solemn purpose is the villanelle, a borrowed lyric form that has been strikingly successful in English. This French-derived (and Italian-originating) form is a classic example of a form whose virtuosity has been adopted as a formal challenge, much favoured in poetry workshops. Since its origins its demanding repetitive form has been found apt for lighter verse, something which makes it remarkable that two of the greatest modern elegies in English are in that echoing form, Dylan Thomas's 'Do Not Go Gentle Into That Good Night', and Elizabeth Bishop's 'One Art'.

> Do not go gentle into that good night.
> Old age should burn and rave at close of day;
> Rage, rage against the dying of the light...
>
> And you, my father, there on that sad height,
> Curse, bless me now with your fierce tears, I pray.
> Do not go gentle into that good night.
> Rage, rage against the dying of the light.

Bishop's poem works to a tragic conclusion, mourning her partner who died by suicide, but in this case the earlier parts of the poem have a misleading lightness which is more characteristic of the villanelle:

> The art of losing isn't hard to master;
> so many things seem filled with the intent
> to be lost that their loss is no disaster.
>
> Lose something every day. Accept the fluster
> of lost door keys, the hour badly spent.
> The art of losing isn't hard to master...

But the ending is far from light:

> —Even losing you (the joking voice, a gesture
> I love) I shan't have lied. It's evident
> the art of losing's not too hard to master
> though it may look like (*Write* it!) like disaster.

The last line takes a devastating turn after the poem has operated with a colloquialism ('losing isn't hard', 'losing's not hard') associated with less sombre occasions. With the two villanelles we might say that their tragic employment of a light, virtuoso form is another instance of the departure from norms noted in several contexts throughout this book, as the genre's expectation is transcended.

It is not only for bereavement that poetry can provide consolation. Adrienne Rich sees the poet as serving a similar consolatory function for the living, 'endowed to speak for those who do not have the gift of language, or to see for those who—for whatever reasons—are less conscious of what they are living through'. Increasingly in his later poetry Seamus Heaney returned to the plight of the 'disregarded' as something the poet must address. His beautiful poem 'Mint' ends by saying that this plant, 'almost beneath notice', is

> Like the disregarded ones we turned against
> Because we'd failed them by our disregard.

And in his free translation of Horace, written to commemorate 9/11, one of the most significant occasional poems of our time, Heaney's figure for the world turned upside down, as well as the tallest towers overturned, is 'those in high places daunted, | Those overlooked regarded'.

This category, with its capacity to comfort and to express generally felt emotions in regular forms, has been called 'wisdom poetry'. Of the major acknowledged elegies in English, one, Thomas Gray's 'Elegy in a Country Churchyard', is not an elegy in the sense of a lament for the death of a particular person at all; it has been called 'universal satire' in the Horatian sense: a reflection on transience in general, expressed through a series of generalizations. Probably no other poem in English has generated so many titles of works in various arts: 'The paths of glory lead but to the grave'; 'Full many a gem of purest ray serene | The dark unfathom'd caves of ocean bear'. English seems to have had a penchant for such general truths from the first: the Anglo-Saxon *Wanderer* begins:

> Often the solitary waits for mercy
> For a lord's favour…
>   Fate stands wholly relentless.

These poems in the *Exeter Book* are usually called elegies; but their gift for general truth makes the alternative term 'consolation' more appropriate, as for Gray's 'Elegy'.

Chapter 5
Poets and readers

'The poet': 'gifted craftsperson'—or everybody?

In the year 2000 Kathleen Raine wrote:

> In the course of my lifetime, poets have ceased to be seen as masters
> of a great art, speaking in the name of some vision of beauty or
> wisdom. Poetry is something everybody writes, interchangeable,
> demotic, involving neither skill nor knowledge but only a
> sufficiently strong urge to write it.

The new order of things of which Raine clearly disapproves
is the notion of poetry as therapy or recreation we have just
looked at. But if the poet is such a masterly individual as
Raine prefers and so much out of the ordinary, might we
ask where their inspiration comes from? The claim for
exceptionalism was expressed very strongly by George Eliot
in *Middlemarch*:

> To be a poet is to have a soul so quick to discern that no shade of
> quality escapes it, and so quick to feel, that discernment is but a
> hand playing with finely ordered variety on the chords of
> emotion—a soul in which knowledge passes instantaneously into
> feeling, and feeling flashes back as a new organ of knowledge.
> One may have that condition by fits only.

We can recognize that what Eliot is expressing is the exalted view of poetry. The contrasting views of the poet at issue here have become particularly contentious in the era of creative writing and poetry workshops, where poetry is regarded as a comforting resource of the kind considered at the end of Chapter 4, or a recreation: both functions which it is often found to perform very well. It comes about perhaps as a by-product of the idea that language—the medium in which the poet works, as distinct from more specializing plastic media like iron or paint or wood or stone—is one that all people employ: whose employment indeed might be seen as the general definition of being human. The poet, then, is a specialist in something that everybody does.

The underlying counter-truth here, as Raine sees it, is expressed in the much-quoted Latin aphorism *Poeta nascitur non fit*: the poet, as master of a great art, is born, not made (the exact source of the Latin aphorism is not known). In English the idea is given authority, but also qualified, by Ben Jonson's lines in his poem 'To the memory of my beloved, The Author Mr William Shakespeare: *and what he hath left us*': he

> Who casts to write a living line, must sweat,
> (Such as thine are) and strike the second heat
> Upon the *Muses* anvile: turne the same,
> (And himself with it) that he thinks to frame;
> Or for the lawrell, he may gain a scorne,
> For a good *Poet*'s made, as well as borne.

The poet also needs to take pains: to revise and polish with a second application of heat. And the Muse here is not a simple inspiration, but provides an anvil, like a blacksmith's, or a potter's wheel. Jonson's view has to be seen too in the context of the Elizabethan debate about seriousness in poetry; here (in *Discoveries*) he is arguing for the poet as a dedicated artificer, not one of the 'rakehelly rout' of poetasters deplored by the Puritans, mentioned in the Introduction here.

But Jonson concedes that the poet has to be born as poet first. Though Shakespeare's 'Art' must 'enjoy a part' in his work, 'Nature her selfe was proud of his designes'. In the *Poetics*, immediately after declaring rhythm to be the second 'cause' of poetry, Aristotle too acknowledges the exceptional status of the poet, in a passage that probably lies behind Jonson's distinction. 'Persons, starting with this natural gift developed by degrees their special aptitudes, till their rude improvisations gave birth to Poetry.' And, just as there are endless considerations of the question 'what is poetry?' we find frequent returns to the question 'what is a poet?' Emerson's 1844 essay, mentioned in the Introduction, is called 'The Poet', but under that heading he considers many of the more general issues about poetry that have been dwelt on here.

The status and nature of 'the poet' has been a weighty matter in English. Keats's letters are often returned to in this discussion, precisely because Keats does not pronounce on the *what* of poetry or the poet, but speaks of life and human experience, and 'the holiness of the heart's emotions', bringing in poetry—and poems—in passing. 'Poetry should be great and unobtrusive, a thing that enters into one's soul, and does not startle it or amaze it with itself but with its subject.—How beautiful are the retired flowers! How would they lose their beauty were they to throng into the highway crying out, "admire me I am a violet! Dote upon me I am a primrose!"' Keats, recognizing the relative failure of *Endymion*, said, 'I would sooner fail than not be among the greatest'.

Poets have to be ambitious, but they must earn the acclaim their art warrants. In his brilliant essays on poets and artists in *The Strength of Poetry*, James Fenton quotes from this same letter—the letter where Keats warns against didactic or opinionated poetry: 'We hate poetry that has a palpable design upon us'—before going on to the pressing question of how success in poetry is earned. Once again the musical parallel is invoked: eminence in music is attained through training and practice, but 'it is far from clear how we are supposed to *earn* success in poetry. Poetry often seems unearned.' Fenton says 'poetry' is earned here—not just *success* in poetry: poetry itself often seems unearned—not just the name of poet. And there has been a good deal of sentimental discussion of the 'found' poem: a piece of language from a different context that is suddenly recognized as having an application in poetry.

The poet and the poem's first person

While taking due account of what poets like Jonson, Keats, Marianne Moore, and Fenton say about poetry outside their own poems, we must recognize that the poet is not necessarily—or all that often—the narrating voice in a poem. It may be of course; a poem like Ben Jonson's desolating 'On My First Son' is clearly more powerful if we take the mourning voice to be that of Ben Jonson himself, when he calls the dead boy 'Ben Jonson his best piece of poetry'. But it is not always possible to be certain because, as Jakobson famously said, often of its nature 'the lyric is in the first person singular'. But this doesn't mean that the first person in the lyric is always to be identified with the poet.

But there are poems—many poems—where we know that the first person of the poem, the 'I' voice, either is or is not the poet. To take one example of each: in Wilfrid Wilson Gibson's poem 'Flannan Isle', the first person 'we' of the poem does not mean Gibson and some other unnamed associates. We know this because in real life Gibson was not a sea safety officer, like the narrator of the poem who describes the journey 'to find out what strange thing might ail | The keepers of the deep-sea light'. The Gothic story is presumably not a real event either: the apparent transformation of three lighthouse keepers into huge black birds, 'Too big by far … For guillemot or shag'. So we are not really concerned with the actual identity of the narrator. He is what is called in prose fiction an unreliable narrator—one of a much more straightforward kind than what that phrase usually implies. But

Poets and readers

this kind of narrative has no intent to deceive: there is no fear of identifying this narrator with the poet.

Poems where the 'I' is positively not to be identified with the writer are the 'dramatic monologues' of Robert Browning. 'My Last Duchess' begins:

> That's my last duchess painted on the wall,
> Looking as if she were alive.

For the sinister, unstated story behind the poem to work, it is essential that the speaking voice be distanced from the poet and the poem. Porphyria's creepy lover in his poem says:

> I found
> A thing to do, and all her hair
> In one long yellow string I wound
> Three times her little throat around,
> And strangled her.

Browning's dramatic monologues have found several distinguished followers in the 20th century. In 'Goldilocks' the London-based Scottish poet Mick Imlah complicates his fictitious narrative by reflecting on what would happen if the Glaswegian tramp the poem's privileged narrator is kicking out of his college room realized that he 'was Scottish!' As with Browning, we don't quite know how to judge this unselfexamining narrator.

There are many poems though where, as in the Ben Jonson elegy, the meaning and success of the poem depend on our identifying the first person: often indeed identifying that voice with the poet. When Yeats begins 'Among School Children' with 'I walk through the long schoolroom questioning', and soon describes himself as 'A sixty-year-old smiling public man', it would be perverse to say we are not sure if this means the poet himself. Yeats was sixty-three, and we know that he visited

St Otteran's School in Waterford on an occasion such as the poem describes. He tells us himself that this was the occasion of the poem. Similarly, Lorna Goodison's poem 'My Great-Grandmother Was a Guinea-Woman' is reporting a biographical fact that is borne out by her *Memoir*. Verse-letters, such as Keats's letter to Reynolds beginning 'Dear Reynolds, as last night I lay in bed', are clear cases of the authorial poem.

Is there an identifiable formal difference between these poems though? Poems like 'Among School Children' when the poet is speaking in his own voice; 'Flannan Isle' where we are sure that he is not; and Muldoon's 'Pancho Villa' where we are not sure? There may in fact be a kind of sliding scale, from poems where it is essential that we recognize the poet as the speaker, to ones where it is crucial that we see the speaker is not the poet: in a Browning monologue, say. It is important that we do not think Bishop Blougram speaks for Browning, or that the sinister narrator of 'My Last Duchess' has authorial validation.

I want to end this part of the discussion with a famously haunting Keats masterpiece:

> This living hand, now warm and capable
> Of earnest grasping, would, if it were cold
> And in the icy silence of the tomb,
> So haunt thy days and chill thy dreaming nights
> That thou wouldst wish thine own heart dry of blood
> So in my veins red life might stream again,
> And thou be conscience-calmed. See here it is—
> I hold it towards you.

It is a compelling biographical case. It used to be suggested, bearing in mind the poet's early death, that the poem was addressed to Fanny Brawne, telling her how terrible she will feel when the poet's death, which he anticipated with his medical knowledge, has come to pass. Readers in the modern era have doubted this. W. Jackson Bate, in his 1963 study *John Keats*, says—less attractively maybe—'the general feeling now is that the lines were a passage he might have intended to use in some future poem or play'. We don't know of course. There is no definite directive from the poet—as there is, say, in Ted Hughes's *Birthday Letters* about his life with Sylvia Plath, or in Robert Lowell's *Life Studies*.

However, in this case it is not simply one thing or the other. 'This Living Hand' has great resonance in the context of Keats's imminent death, whatever exactly his intention was for this fragment that he wrote on the margin of another (very different) poem. As it happens, the dead hand of the poem has an odd resonance from a very sinister haunting poem by John Donne, 'The Apparition', in which a rejected lover threatens to return to haunt the beloved while she is in the act of love with someone else. This may be mnemonic irrelevance (an important possibility in poetry too of course); but, once the thought and link have come into the reader's mind, it is impossible to dismiss it. It remains what has been called an intertextual presence.

The strictures of the New Critics, often salutary in their time, against 'intentionalist' readings which drew on extra-textual evidence from a writer's life and times, can now seem at best limited and at worst cripplingly doctrinaire. It seems from most of the cases we have looked at that it is not possible to tell formally whether the poet is the same as the narrator, and whether either (or both) is the first person voice in the poem. As the French poet Arthur Rimbaud famously said, '*je est un autre*': 'I is not I'—not necessarily anyway. And the further back in time the poem is, the more difficult it is to be certain. We have many avenues to turn to in trying to establish the meaning of a 21st-century poem. It is harder to be sure about what Chaucer is driving at. (Already, a mere hundred years after his own time, the Scottish poet Henryson was wondering 'who knows if all that Chaucer wrote is true?')

In practice we have to make our mind up: to make a judgement about the voice we are listening to as we read. If we didn't, we wouldn't be able to conclude anything from the poem at all. We wouldn't, in any full sense, understand it. What we are doing in part is making a judgement about the genre of the poem, a judgement which is central to understanding. If we deduce, as we well might, from the tone of the opening of King Lear—'I thought the King had more affected the Duke of Albany than Cornwall'—that we are embarking on a comedy or a straightforward history play (if there is such a genre), we will not have to read much further before we realize it is far from comic: once we have seen the terrible, angry dénouement of that scene, we would have to start again on a more secure generic footing.

There is a case where we can resolve the matter, it might seem: when the author is still there to be asked. The start of John Fuller's poem 'Pyrosymphonie' has a wonderfully haunting power if we read it as addressed to his lifelong, deeply loved wife:

> You and I, when our days are done, must say
> Without exactly saying it, goodbye.

If it is not addressed to his wife, the poem is altogether harder to locate—and less emotionally forceful. Who else do you say goodbye to, without exactly saying it? Someone when they die, certainly: but this makes much less of the 'you and I'. We should if possible, without being unduly intentionalist, take the reading which most enriches the impact of the poem.

I imagine though in this case if we asked the author if this is what he meant—as we could, and as we could have asked Keats while he was still alive—he would say something like: 'yes, I suppose so. But other things too.' A famous passage by T. S. Eliot addresses this: in the Conclusion to his *The Use of Poetry and the Use of Criticism* (1933), a book which is concerned with two questions, 'What is Poetry?' and 'Is this a good poem?', Eliot says that poetic

119

intensity often derives from 'feelings too obscure for the authors even to know quite what they were.... Why, for all of us, out of all that we have heard, seen, felt, in a lifetime, do certain images recur, charged with emotion, rather than others?'

In the early to mid-20th century the New Critics, among whom Eliot was a leader, treated the poem as a free-standing item which, once it had come into being by whatever means, was completely free of its producer or any wider contexts. It was a kind of sacrilege to make any kind of claim or observation beyond what was made explicit in the written form. There are many stories, real as well as apocryphal no doubt, about poets disowning responsibility for interpretation of their own writing. When Eliot was asked what was the meaning of the first line of his poem 'Ash Wednesday'—'Lady, three white leopards sat under a juniper-tree'—he replied, 'it means "Lady, three white leopards sat under a juniper-tree"'. A famous instance of this abjuration of authority, before the more questioning era of modernism or the New Critics' reverence before the text, is the apocryphal-sounding story of Robert Browning who, when asked the meaning of a poem of his, replied, 'When I wrote it, only God and Robert Browning knew what it meant. Now only God knows.'

In a celebrated essay title deploring intentionalism—the critical practice of speculating about what the writer meant, beyond what it says on the page—L. C. Knights offered the question 'How Many Children had Lady Macbeth?' as an example of the sort of question that should not be raised because its answer was not to be found in the text. But is this so unworthy or trivial a question? Lady Macbeth says she has 'given suck' and would dash her nipple from her child's 'boneless gums' if she had sworn to. And why does Macbeth become so agitated about the idea that Banquo's children will succeed to the throne, not his? The Macbeths must have at least one child it seems. And the fact that we can't answer Knights's question can't stop our minds wandering to it. Gerard Manley Hopkins wrote a witty

intentionalist 'Triolet' on Wordsworth's 'The Rainbow', suggesting
'what the poet really did write':

> 'The child is father to the man'.
> How can he be? The words are wild.
> Suck any sense from that who can:
> 'The child is father to the man.'
> No; what the poet did write ran,
> 'The man is father to the child.'
> 'The child is father to the man'!
> How *can* he be? The words are wild.

The 'intentional fallacy' developed a much more secure foundation
with Jacques Derrida who said there is no '*hors-texte*'. If that is the
case presumably any question beyond the immediate literal
context of the poem is as good as any other. Perhaps the most
famous modern statement of the dilemma of deciding is Robert
Lowell's 'Epilogue', the last poem in his last book, *Day by Day*,
in 1977:

> Those blessed structures, plot and rhyme—
> why are they no help to me now
> I want to make
> something imagined, not recalled?
> I hear the noise of my own voice:
> *The painter's vision is not a lens,*
> *it trembles to caress the light.*
> But sometimes everything I write
> with the threadbare art of my eye
> seems a snapshot,
> lurid, rapid, garish, grouped,
> heightened from life,
> yet paralyzed by fact.
> All's misalliance.
> Yet why not say what happened?

Pray for the grace of accuracy
Vermeer gave to the sun's illumination
stealing like the tide across a map
to his girl solid with yearning.
We are poor passing facts,
warned by that to give
each figure in the photograph
his living name.

Readers and critics

Next, the question of audience: who are these poetic voices
addressing themselves to? Shelley said, 'A poet is a nightingale,
who sits in darkness and sings to cheer its own solitude with sweet
sounds; his auditors are as men entranced by the melody of an
unseen musician, who feel that they are moved and softened, yet
know not whence or why.' Frost too saw readership as a response
to sound: 'The ear is the only true writer and the only true reader.'
Despite his New Critic's insistence on the inscrutable independence
of the written poem, T. S. Eliot also defined the lyric as 'the voice
of the poet talking to himself—or to nobody'. So who is it that poetry
is addressed to? Walt Whitman said 'Great Poetry is possible only
if there are great readers'. In the later 20th century the critics of
the movement called 'reception theory' placed a new emphasis on
the reader as the realizer of the poem at least as much as the poet.
But what would a great reader be?

All our serious reading, especially of poetry, is provisional.
Everyone must have had the feeling that the reading they are
doing at the moment is a dry run, a practice, for an ideal reading
that we will return to. If we didn't think something like this, we
would never finish reading anything because we would keep
going back over what we were reading now to be sure we were
getting the total sense of it. With narrative we don't reread in
this way because we wouldn't keep the story moving in a
productive way.

The art historian Wilhelm Worringer makes a critical distinction between empathy and abstraction (enlighteningly applied to music by Anthony Storr). To enjoy a work of art, the observer must empathize with it and be emotionally involved in it. But an abstract aesthetic appreciation draws on knowledge of form: a sense of the 'Blessed rage for order' that Wallace Stevens celebrates in 'The Idea of Order at Key West'. In application to poetry, one might say that the empathetic reader says 'I don't know much about poetry; but I know what I like', while the scholarly abstracting critic reads or hears poetry with a presupposing technical knowledge.

Mostly, of course, except when we are reading as scholars (and often even then), we do not return to make an ideal reading. Most of us who read poetry probably feel that we will return to read *Paradise Lost* at some point. Some of us will; but most won't. This is because it is long; we won't return to it as a whole because we are treating it as a long narrative. But reading short poems is not like this. As when we do a translation from a foreign language—what used to be called an 'unseen'—our first reading is entirely exploratory and wool gathering, but we know we will go back immediately to read through again.

The universally enjoyed practice of 'close reading' is the application of some kinds of knowledge and expectations in approaching a poem: various attempts were made in the 20th century to put criticism of poetry on a more scientific footing. One now infamous example of a poem-unlocking system was set out by Denys Thompson in his book *Reading and Discrimination* in 1934. Thompson proposed the acronym SIFT—sense, intention, feeling, tone—for the four factors that I. A. Richards said might be looked for in a poem. (Two of them—intention and feeling—are among the fallacies deplored by W. K. Wimsatt in his influential book *The Verbal Icon*, which is best remembered for identifying the intentionalist fallacy and the affective fallacy. The latter fallacy corresponds to the empathetic aesthetic outlined by Worringer.)

So the principles of criticism—opposed to poetry by T. S. Eliot—are as debated as the definitions of poetry itself. What kind of criticism or reading we practise depends on what we think poetry is and what it is for: the questions this book began with. And we might finally allay the uncertainty of that debate by recalling again what Wallace Stevens said: that it is not poetry itself, but the exploration of what poetry is that is such an enhancement of life.

Conclusion

Having started with grand claims for poetry, by Shelley, Wallace Stevens, and others, on grounds of public utility, this brief consideration of what poetry is has encountered a series of recurrent features. Its primary effect seems to be to satisfy what the reader or hearer wants by surprising them in some way. It is never the statement of the obvious. It may be abnormal in language or in opinion or in organization. But it must not be abnormal for the sake of it; it must not be perverse, because its endeavour is to expose the truth in some sense that is not obvious. It works in the service of reality. It is in that sense that it is an enhancement of life as we end where we began.

Further reading

Modern introductions and discussions

Agamben, Giorgio, *The End of the Poem: Studies in Poetics* (Stanford University Press, 1999).

Attridge, Derek, *Peculiar Language* (Routledge, 1988, reprinted 2004).

Attridge, Derek, *Poetic Rhythm: An Introduction* (Cambridge University Press, 1995).

Boland, Eavan and M. Strand, eds, *The Making of a Poem: A Norton Anthology of Poetic Forms* (Norton, 2001).

Brooke-Rose, Christine, *A Grammar of Metaphor* (Secker and Warburg, 1958).

Caudwell, Christopher, *Illusion and Reality* (Macmillan, 1937).

Constantine, David, *Poetry*, 'The Literary Agenda' series (Oxford University Press, 2013).

Eagleton, Terry, *How to Read a Poem* (Blackwell, 2007).

Fenton, James, *An Introduction to English Poetry* (Viking, 2002).

Ferry, Anne, *The Title to the Poem* (Stanford University Press, 1996).

Fussell, Paul, *Poetic Meter and Poetic Form* (McGraw-Hill, 1965).

Heaney, Seamus, *The Government of the Tongue* (Faber, 1988).

Hobsbaum, Philip, *Metre, Rhythm and Verse Form* (New Critical Idiom, 1995).

Hollander, John, *Vision and Resonance: Two Senses of Poetic Form* (Oxford University Press, 1975).

Hollander, John, *Rhyme's Reason* (Yale Nota Bene, 2001).

Hollander, John, *The Work of Poetry* (Columbia University Press, 1998).

Lennard, John, *The Poetry Handbook: A Guide to Reading Poetry for Pleasure and Practical Criticism* (Oxford University Press, 1996).

Matterson, Stephen and Darryl Jones, *Studying Poetry* (Arnold, 2000).

Maxwell, Glyn, *On Poetry* (Oberon Masters, 2012).

Muldoon, Paul, *The End of the Poem: Oxford Lectures* (Faber & Faber, 2009).

Parini, Jay, *Why Poetry Matters* (Yale University Press, 2008).

Redmond, John, *How to Write a Poem* (Blackwell, 2006).

Roberts, Phil, *How Poetry Works* (Penguin, 1986).

Sansom, Ian, *The Enthusiast's Field Guide to Poetry* (Quercus, 2007).

Simic, Charles, *The Metaphysician in the Dark* (University of Michigan Press, 2003).

Stevens, Wallace, *The Necessary Angel: Essays on Reality and the Imagination* (Knopf, 1951).

Strachan, John and Richard Terry, *Poetry*, 'Elements of Literature' series (Edinburgh University Press, 2000).

Wainwright, Jeffrey, *Poetry: The Basics* (Routledge, 2004).

Wellek, René and Austin Warren, *Theory of Literature* (Cape, 1949).

Wolosky, Shira, *The Art of Poetry: How to Read a Poem* (Oxford University Press, 2001).

Earlier/classic discussions

Abrams, M. H., *The Mirror and the Lamp* (W. W. Norton, 1953).

Aristotle, *Poetics* (*c.*347–322 BC). See Dorsch (1965).

Auden, W. H., *The Dyer's Hand* (Faber, 1963).

Bateson, F. W., *English Poetry: A Critical Introduction* (Longman, 1950).

Brodsky, Joseph, *On Grief and Reason: Essays* (Penguin, 1995).

Davie, Donald, *Articulate Energy: An Enquiry into the Syntax of English Poetry* (Routledge & Kegan Paul, 1957).

Eco, Umberto, 'The *Poetics* and Us', in *On Literature*, translated by Martin McLaughlin (Vintage Books, 2006).

Emerson, R. W., 'The Poet', in *Essays: Second Series* (Donohue, Henneberry & Co., 1844).

Goethe, *Conversations of Goethe with Johann Peter Eckermann*, translated by John Oxenford (Da Capo Press, 1998).

Graves, Robert, *Poetic Craft and Technique* (Cassell, 1967).

Greene, Ronald, ed., *The Princeton Encyclopedia of Poetry and Poetics*, 4th edition (Princeton University Press, 2012).

Poetry

Hamilton, William Rowan, 'Introductory Lecture on Astronomy', *The Dublin University Review and Quarterly Magazine*, 1 (January 1833), 72–85. https://www.maths.tcd.ie/pub/HistMath/People/Hamilton/Lectures/AstIntro.html

Hawkes, David, 'Literature', in Raymond Dawson, ed., *The Legacy of China* (Clarendon Press, 1964).

Horace, *Art of Poetry*. See Dorsch (1965).

Housman, A. E., *The Name and Nature of Poetry* (Cambridge University Press, 1933).

Jackson, W. R., *The Idea of Lyric: Lyric Modes in Ancient and Modern Poetry* (University of California Press, 1982).

Jakobson, Roman, *Language in Literature* (Harvard University Press, 1987).

Liu, James J. Y., *The Art of Chinese Poetry* (University of Chicago Press, 1962).

Mill, J. S., 'Thoughts on Poetry and its Varieties' (1833).

Plato, *Ion*. See Harmon (2003) (and for *Republic*).

Poe, Edgar Allan, *Poems and Essays on Poetry*, ed. C. S. Sisson (Carcanet, 1995). Note 'The Philosophy of Composition' (pp. 138–50).

Pound, Ezra, *The ABC of Poetry* (Faber, 1951).

Preminger, A. and T. V. F. Brogan, eds, *The Princeton Encyclopedia of Poetry and Poetics* (Princeton University Press, 1993).

Shelley, Percy Bysshe, *A Defence of Poetry* (1821; published 1840).

Sidney, Sir Philip, *An Apologie for Poetry* (1579; published 1595).

Useful anthologies

Dorsch, T. S., *Classical Literary Criticism: Aristotle: On the Art of Poetry; Horace: On the Art of Poetry; Longinus: On the Sublime* (Penguin Books, 1965).

Harmon, William, *Classic Writings on Poetry* (Columbia University Press, 2003).

Laird, Nick and Don Patterson, *The Zoo of the New: Poems to Read Now* (Particular Books, 2017).

McCorkle, James, ed., *Conversant Essays: Contemporary Poets on Poetry* (Wayne State University Press, 1990).

Russell, D. A. and M. Winterbottom, *Classical Literary Criticism* (Oxford University Press, 1989).

Van Doren, Mark, *An Anthology of World Poetry* (Cassell, 1929).

Entertaining discussions

Bishop, Elizabeth, *The Collected Prose*, edited by Robert Giroux (Farrar Straus Giroux, 1985).

Fuller, John, *Who is Ozymandias? And other Puzzles in Poetry* (Chatto, 2011).

Milosz, Czeslaw, *The Witness of Poetry* (Harvard University Press, 1983).

Paulin, Tom, *The Secret Lives of Poems* (Faber, 2008).

Rich, Adrienne, *On Lies, Secrets and Silence* (Virago, 1980).

Storr, Anthony, *Music and the Mind* (HarperCollins, 1992).

Travisano, Thomas and Saskia Hamilton, eds, *Words in Air: The Complete Correspondence Between Elizabeth Bishop and Robert Lowell* (Faber & Faber 2008).

Publisher's acknowledgements

We are grateful for permission to include the following copyright material in this book.

Extract from Arthur Quiller-Couch, ed., 1919. *The Oxford Book of English Verse: 1250–1900.*

Extract from James J. Y. Liu (1962), *The Art of Chinese Poetry.*

World excluding US: 'The Diviner', from *Death of a Naturalist* by Seamus Heaney. Reprinted by permission of Faber and Faber Ltd. US: 'The Diviner', from *Opened Ground: Selected Poems 1966–1996* by Seamus Heaney. Copyright © 1998 by Seamus Heaney. Reprinted by permission of Farrar, Straus and Giroux.

World excluding US: Excerpt from 'Mint' from *New and Selected Poems 1988–2013* by Seamus Heaney. Reprinted by permission of Faber and Faber Ltd. US: Excerpt from 'Mint' from *Opened Ground: Selected Poems 1966–1996* by Seamus Heaney. Copyright © 1998 by Seamus Heaney. Reprinted by permission of Farrar, Straus and Giroux.

US, its territories and dependencies, republic of Philippines and the nonexclusive open market excluding UK and British Commonwealth: Excerpt from 'Anything Can Happen' from *Selected Poems 1988–2013* by Seamus Heaney. Copyright © 2014 by the Estate of Seamus Heaney. Reprinted by permission of Farrar, Straus and Giroux.

Extract from T. S. Eliot (1922), 'The Burial of the Dead' from *The Waste Land*.

UK and British Commonwealth: Excerpt from *Personae* by Ezra Pound. Reprinted by permission of Faber and Faber Ltd. World, including Canada, excluding British Commonwealth: 'In a Station of the Metro' by Ezra Pound, from *Personae*. Copyright © 1926 by Ezra Pound. Reprinted by permission of New Directions Publishing Corp.

Extract from Raymond Dawson, *The Legacy of China* (Boston: Cheng and Tsui Company). Reprinted by arrangement with OUP. Copyright Oxford University Press, 1964, p. 103. By permission of Oxford University Press.

Extract from Adrian Mitchell (1964), preface of *Poems*.

Excerpt from 'God, a poem' from *Yellow Tulips: Poems 1968–2011* by James Fenton. Faber and Faber Ltd.

US, its territories and dependencies, republic of Philippines, Canada: 'Snow White and the Seven Dwarfs' from *Roald Dahl's Revolting Rhymes* by Roald Dahl, text copyright © 1982 by Roald Dahl Nominee Limited. Used by permission of Alfred A. Knopf, an imprint of Random House Children's Books, a division of Penguin Random House LLC. All rights reserved. Other territories: Excerpt from 'Snow White and the Seven Dwarfs'. In *Revolting Rhymes* by Roald Dahl. London, UK: Jonathan Cape Ltd & Penguin Books Ltd.

Excerpt from 'A Martian Sends a Postcard Home' by Craig Raine (1979).

Excerpt from 'Disobedience' by A. A. Milne.

World excluding US, its territories and Canada: excerpt from 'Do not go gentle into that good night' from *The Collected Poems of Dylan Thomas: The Centenary Edition*. Weidenfeld & Nicolson. Reprinted by permission of the Dylan Thomas Trust. US, its territories and Canada: 'Do Not Go Gentle Into That Good Night' by Dylan Thomas, from *The Poems of Dylan Thomas*. Copyright © 1952 by Dylan Thomas.

Index

Index

Index

Index

S

Index

SPANISH LITERATURE
A Very Short Introduction
Jo Labanyi

This *Very Short Introduction* explores the rich literary history of Spanish literature, which resonates with contemporary debates on transnationalism and cultural diversity. The book introduces a general readership to the ways in which Spanish literature has been read, in and outside Spain, explaining misconceptions, outlining the insights of recent scholarship and suggesting new readings. It highlights the precocious modernity of much early modern Spanish literature, and shows how the gap between modern ideas and social reality stimulated creative literary responses in subsequent periods; as well as how contemporary writers have adjusted to Spain's recent accelerated modernization.

Science Fiction
A Very Short Introduction
David Seed

Science Fiction has proved notoriously difficult to define. It has been explained as a combination of romance, science and prophecy; as a genre based on an imagined alternative to the reader's environment; and as a form of fantastic fiction and historical literature. It has also been argued that science fiction narratives are the most engaged, socially relevant, and responsive to the modern technological environment. This *Very Short Introduction* doesn't offer a history of science fiction, but instead ties examples of science fiction to different historical moments, in order to demonstrate how science fiction has evolved over time.

www.oup.com/vsi

WRITING AND SCRIPT
A Very Short Introduction
Andrew Robinson

Without writing, there would be no records, no history, no books, and no emails. Writing is an integral and essential part of our lives; but when did it start? Why do we all write differently and how did writing develop into what we use today? All of these questions are answered in this *Very Short Introduction*. Starting with the origins of writing five thousand years ago, with cuneiform and Egyptian hieroglyphs, Andrew Robinson explains how these early forms of writing developed into hundreds of scripts including the Roman alphabet and the Chinese characters.

'User-friendly survey.'

Steven Poole, The Guardian

ENGLISH LITERATURE

A Very Short Introduction

Jonathan Bate

Sweeping across two millennia and every literary genre, acclaimed scholar and biographer Jonathan Bate provides a dazzling introduction to English Literature. The focus is wide, shifting from the birth of the novel and the brilliance of English comedy to the deep Englishness of landscape poetry and the ethnic diversity of Britain's Nobel literature laureates. It goes on to provide a more in-depth analysis, with close readings from an extraordinary scene in King Lear to a war poem by Carol Ann Duffy, and a series of striking examples of how literary texts change as they are transmitted from writer to reader.

{No reviews}

FRENCH LITERATURE
A Very Short Introduction
John D. Lyons

The heritage of literature in the French language is rich, varied, and extensive in time and space; appealing both to its immediate public, readers of French, and also to a global audience reached through translations and film adaptations. *French Literature: A Very Short Introduction* introduces this lively literary world by focusing on texts - epics, novels, plays, poems, and screenplays - that concern protagonists whose adventures and conflicts reveal shifts in literary and social practices. From the hero of the medieval *Song of Roland* to the Caribbean heroines of *Tituba, Black Witch of Salem* or the European expatriate in Japan in *Fear and Trembling*, these problematic protagonists allow us to understand what interests writers and readers across the wide world of French.

GLOBALIZATION
A Very Short Introduction
Manfred Steger

'Globalization' has become one of the defining buzzwords of our time - a term that describes a variety of accelerating economic, political, cultural, ideological, and environmental processes that are rapidly altering our experience of the world. It is by its nature a dynamic topic - and this *Very Short Introduction* has been fully updated for 2009, to include developments in global politics, the impact of terrorism, and environmental issues. Presenting globalization in accessible language as a multifaceted process encompassing global, regional, and local aspects of social life, Manfred B. Steger looks at its causes and effects, examines whether it is a new phenomenon, and explores the question of whether, ultimately, globalization is a good or a bad thing.